Finding Mercy

BOOK TWO: FORBIDDEN DESIRES OF PCH SERIES

CHELLE ROSE

To rechargeable vibrators...
May you not die during the reading of this book.

Finding Mercy

By Chelle Rose

"Hearts will never be practical until they are made unbreakable."

Please note for those of you that had trouble with the cancer storyline in book one it's much less of one in this book.

Stay up to date on all of my new releases by joining my Facebook readers group: Facebook Reader's Group

Finding Mercy © 2022

Chelle Rose, Author

This book is a work of fiction. Names, characters, places, and incidents are the product of the author's imagination or are used fictitiously. Any resemblance to actual events, locations, or persons, living or dead, is coincidental. This book is intended for a mature audience 18+. There may be some violence, drug use, or other triggers. Please be aware if you have any of those triggers.

Printed in the United States of America

Cover by: Ctrl. Alt. Publish.

Edited by: Shel's Editing Services

One

LIAM

"WHERE THE FUCK IS SHE?"

My eyes snap up and I spot Gilbert, Mercy's father, standing before me.

"I didn't do it."

"Then who the fuck did? Where's my fucking daughter, Liam? My wife is going to go out of her mind. She has already lost one daughter."

I blow out a long breath.

"My son kidnapped Mercy. They think she's dead. But she can't be."

He grabs onto the bars, squeezing tight, turning his knuckles white, he's seething, as he should be. After all, he may be an asshole, but he is still her father. "I need you to help me find her. I know you have connections," I say.

"Why would your son kidnap my daughter?"

I sigh as I tell him the whole sordid situation.

"When I find my daughter, and I will, you do realize, I'm going to put a bullet in your son's brain, right?"

I shake my head and ball up my fists, "You owe me a favor."

He glares at me, "What are you asking here?"

"Find her. Let the police deal with my son. I don't want him to die.

He's a troubled young man not a monster. But, if you can't save her without killing him, then you do what you need to do."

With pinched eyebrows, he says, "You do realize, if I grant this favor, you'll owe me? You will be in my debt, and I will collect on that debt."

I run my hands through my hair, "I don't care. Find Mercy, save my son. You can take my life; it doesn't matter to me."

"I won't take your life, Mercy would never forgive me, as tempting as it is."

I nod because I know he's right. She loves me like no other woman ever has. I miss her so much, and the thought of never seeing her again, leaves a lump in my throat and an ache in my chest. Even thinking I will never hold her again sends me into a dark pit of devastation.

"Her condition will dictate your debt. Now, do you have any idea where he has her?"

I rub my jaw in contemplation, "Not a clue. He's a drug addict, so wherever you can find drugs you'll find him."

"Do you think he's capable of taking her life?"

I start to pace, "I don't know. I wouldn't have thought he was the type of person to kidnap her, and he did. The drugs have taken over at this point. My son has turned into someone I don't even know."

In a split-second decision, I decided to keep to myself, he plans on raping her. That's not something a father needs to know.

"What kind of drugs?"

"I don't know. Something hard obviously. I asked, but he never told me what he was using."

He pulls out a notepad and pen from his back pants pocket.

"What's his name?"

"Nash Lexington."

"I'll be in contact, but please know, if I find out you're lying to me, and you had anything to do with this, I will kill you regardless of what Mercy wants."

"I understand. I would never hurt her."

He sighs, "I believe you. I'm going to call in a favor and try to get you out of here today."

"Thank you."

Putting his hands in his pockets, he says, "It's not for you. You're going to help me find her. I swear to you if I have to tell my wife she has lost another daughter I just might kill you both."

He hands me a piece of paper, "Call me when you get out, at this phone number. Do not use my personal number. I'm going to go talk to a few of my informants and see if I can find anything out."

As he leaves, I breathe a sigh of relief, finally someone who can and will help me. He must have some pretty great connections because an hour later, I meet privately with a judge and am granted bail. As I leave my cell, I get many a glare and sighs front he officers. But none of that matters. I care about one thing, finding my girl.

After collecting my cell phone, wallet, and keys, I head out to the street and call Xander to come get me. But he's in surgery, so I call Gilbert and ask where I should meet him. He tells me to wait at the corner of Seventh and Mountaintop and he'll send a car. We are meeting at a bar in Stroudsburg, which makes sense because there are a lot of drugs in that area. Luckily, it's only a thirty-five-minute drive so it won't take long. I'm itching to find Mercy and make sure she's safe. A black Escalade pulls up after what feels like forever. He rolls the window down and asks, "Liam?" I nod and open the back door and slide in.

I have hope for the first time since I walked into my house and found her missing. We are going to find her. And when I do, I'm installing a surveillance system, video cameras fucking everywhere. Hell, I may never let her out of my sight ever again.

I love you, baby girl, please hold on.

When we arrive, I rush into the bar where I'm meeting Gilbert. He's sitting in a corner booth with a young man that I immediately recognize. Nash's friend Matt sits with him. I walk up to them and sit down, "What the fuck are you doing here?"

Matt sits in the booth, his eyes staring down at the table, as he trembles uncontrollably.

Gilbert narrows his eyes, "Matt here was just admitting to me that he's your son's drug dealer."

Instantly, I see red and want to pound this fuckers face in. But I tell myself, this is about Mercy. You can deal with the rest later. Mercy. That's it. But fuck he owns some responsibility in this. He has been friends with Nash since they were little kids. How could he give drugs to him? Why is he even involved in drugs? Matt comes from a good, religious family. Hell, his father is a priest of an Episcopalian church.

"Did you know he took her?"

"Yeah," he averts my gaze.

"Where the fuck are they?" I almost yell.

Gilbert points his finger down, "Calm the fuck down. You aren't helping."

Shaking his head, Matt says, "I really don't know."

Gilbert glares at him with his hands on the edge of the table in a death grip, "You don't want to go to jail today or worse, right?"

What's worse than jail? Will he actually kill him? Probably. This is not your *to serve and protect* type of cop.

Matt peers up at him, "No."

"Good. Then you're going to help us find her. When are you seeing Nash? I assume he'll need drugs."

He shakes his head, "I told him no more. He's gone insane; besides, he has no money."

"How do you contact him?" Gilbert asks.

Mumbling he responds, "Cell. He's got a burner phone now."

A waitress walks over to our table, but Gilbert holds up his hand and she turns on her heel and walks away without another glance.

"Text him. Tell him you will give him a little bit, this one last time."

"Right now?"

Gilbert glares at him so hard, I think he might catch on fire. "Yes, now, you fucking idiot."

He gets out his cell phone and sends a text while I say a silent prayer.

His phone starts ringing almost immediately, "It's Nash."

"Get proof of life," he says, "I need to know my daughter is alive."

He presses the answer button, "Hey man."

As he talks, he looks at Gilbert and then at me, "It's only been two days since I gave you the last batch. How can you be so sick already?"

Matt huffs, "Alright, I got you. I'll give you enough to take the edge off. But you're going to have to get me some cash soon or you'll be dope sick all over again."

"Okay, I'll be at our meeting spot in under an hour, but Nash? Tell me you didn't kill her? I've been sick thinking about it. She's my friend too." He moves the phone away so we can hear.

"Baby, tell him you're alive." Nash's voice comes through the phone.

Mercy cries out, "I wish I were dead."

I cover my mouth to hide the sob trying to escape.

Nash laughs, "I thought we were having so much fun together, my little whore."

I clench my fists under the table when I hear Nash calling her his and a whore. Neither sit well with me. He better not have fucking raped her.

Matt says, "Nash, please don't hurt her. I'll be there soon."

"Alright," Matt says and disconnects the call.

"He says he's not far from the meeting spot, so he wants me to text him when I get there. It's a two-minute walk, so she can't be far and she's alive."

Alive is great, trust me, I'm relieved. But at what cost? What has he done to her? And how long will it take her to recover? Will she recover from something like this? She's strong but even steel can break. I keep hearing her scream, *'I wish I were dead'*, on repeat in my head. What has he done to my girl to make her wish for death?

Two

LIAM

"THIS IS how this is going to work. Matt is going to go by himself, so we don't spook your kid. Matt, you are not to give up any drugs without seeing Mercy first. Liam, you will stay in this bar until I text you. Once I see where they go you will hear from me. Until then, you stay put." He glances back and forth between us before glaring at me.

I shake my head, "No. I'll go with you."

He slams his fist on the table, "Oh, the good doctor has experience with stakeouts? Following people while remaining unseen?"

"No, of course not," I admit.

"*And* that is exactly why you will follow my fucking orders."

I nod because what else can I even say? I don't want to stay back, I hate waiting. But he's right, this is most definitely out of my expertise.

Glancing at Matt I ask, "What kind of drugs is he on?"

He swallows hard, "Heroin and Fentanyl."

"Jesus."

Hanging his head low he speaks in a shaky voice, "Dr. Lexington, I'm sorry."

I want to throttle this fucking kid but instead say, "If anything happens to Mercy or my son you will be sorry. So, fucking sorry."

Matt's phone chimes, "He said five minutes."

Gilbert stands, "Alright let's get in place. I'll watch to see where you go. Liam, be ready for my text."

Matt stands and walks, followed by Gilbert. Maybe it's his police training but he seems so detached. It seems like it's just a job to him, not like his daughter has been fucking kidnapped. I hate this fucker.

I put money on the table so I can leave the second I hear from him. Holding my phone in my hand, I stare at the screen waiting.

Mercy, please be okay. My mind is fucking racing with dark thoughts about the state we may find her in. What the hell was he thinking? And what has he done to her? When this day is done, he will either be dead or going to prison while my girl, I have no idea what's going to happen to her. Fuck, I hope he hasn't hurt her. But I know the odds of that are slim to none. He hurt her before, and now that he has her alone it could only be worse. She's going to hate me, after all, he's, my son. I hate myself for not seeing this sooner. And why the hell did I not change the lock code? If I had, this wouldn't be happening. It's my fault, I am to blame. How can she possibly look at me after this? My chest tightens as my phone lights up with a text message from Gilbert.

Left side of the courtyard behind the statue.

I get up and open the door, walking to Gilbert, my hands shake uncontrollably. Gilbert speaks without looking at me, "That abandoned building straight ahead, that's where they are. Luckily for us, the windows are boarded so he won't see you coming." He continues, "Let's go. It's time to save Mercy." He pulls out his gun.

"You said you wouldn't kill him."

Shaking his head, he speaks through a clenched jaw, "I said I'd try not to kill him. I made no guarantees. Fucking deal with it."

Fuck I hate this guy. I may have just given my son a death sentence. But what choice did I have?

The tension is palpable as we walk into the building, neither of us quite sure what's going to happen in the scene that's about to unfold before us. My breathing is heavy as we walk through the door, anxiety clawing at my chest.

I hear her before I see her, sobbing, begging Nash.

"Please don't do this to me."

Matt pleads, "Dude. Fuck. Stop. Don't do this."

We turn left following their voices. When we walk into the room, I realize nothing could have ever prepared me for what I'm looking at. All the air escapes my lungs as I see my son holding Mercy's hands above her head, her wrists tight in his grip. She's naked, he has her legs spread as his cock is at her entrance. Matt cowers in the corner of the room covering his face with his hands unable to watch the situation he helped create.

"Son, this is the drugs, this is not the man I raised. Let her go. Don't do this." I try to sound calm but inside I'm panicking. In seconds, I could be watching my son rape my girl. Or I could watch Gilbert blow his brains across the room.

Gilbert moves to Nash and puts the gun to the back of his head.

"Get the fuck off her before I fucking end you."

How can everything move in fast motion and slow motion at the same exact time? Everything is a fucking blur. My son on top of Mercy fully intending to rape her. Gilbert with a gun to the back of my son's head. I want to run to her, I want to run to him and stop Gilbert from killing him, I want to do something, but I can't fucking move. My legs are like lead beneath me barely able to hold my weight. Neither of them have moved in what feels like the longest time. Then I hear Gilbert cock the firearm in his hands. He slides the top back; it makes a loud clanging noise and pulls me from my panicked state.

I run to them as Nash releases her hands and she scoots backwards to the head of the mattress frantic. Gilbert pistol whips him, Nash collapses, falling to the floor. Gilbert holds him in place with his boot on his throat. Taking off my suit jacket, I reach out to cover Mercy.

She pulls her knees to her chest, wrapping her arms around herself. She attempts to back away from me when her back hits the wall behind her. "Please stay away from me. Go away, Liam," she says in a broken voice.

My heart shatters into a million fucking pieces as I attempt to digest her words.

"Baby girl, come here. We have to get you off that filthy mattress. It's an infection waiting to happen."

She shakes her head as she trembles like a fucking leaf.

Her voice is shaky as she whispers, "It's over Liam. Leave me alone."

Tears fall from her eyes, and I want to kiss the wetness away. I want to make this better, but I can't.

"You heard her, it's time to leave her alone."

Nash cries out in harsh pants, "I can't breathe."

Gilbert cackles, "As if I fucking care!"

Gilbert makes a call to have someone come and arrest my son for kidnapping and attempted rape.

"Are you sure?" I ask Mercy.

As tears roll down my face she nods, "Yes."

She glances at me and quickly looks away as if pained by the mere sight of me.

"I love you, baby girl."

I glance at Gilbert, "We have a deal."

He nods.

"Matt, get the fuck out before the police get here. You're lucky. You get to live today. I'll be in contact. You fucking owe me," Gilbert barks.

I throw my jacket over her legs and do the hardest fucking thing I've ever done in my life; I leave. Leaving my heart and soul in that room. As I walk out to the street looking for a cab, I'm having trouble accepting her words. No, she'll be back, I tell myself. When she comes to pick up her things from my house, I'll make her see how much I love her, how much I need her. Then she'll change her mind. This is temporary. Then I hear a little voice in my head. *What if it's not? What if you've lost her?* Did my son just cost me everything good in my life? Mercy is everything good in my life. Without her it's all just gray, none of it matters.

My phone has been ringing for a while. I climb into the cab and give the driver my address and answer my phone since it's Xander.

"What?" I answer.

"Where are you?"

"In Stroudsburg on my way home."

He sighs, "Are you alright, Liam?"

"Nope," I answer and hang up. I'm not in the mood to talk about this shit in the back of a cab for this asshole to listen in on. I slide my ringing phone back in my pocket. I shouldn't have answered it the first time. When we pull into my driveway, I immediately spot Xander sitting on my porch.

I get out of the cab and walk up to my porch ignoring the giant man sitting there. I walk around him and go inside and of course he follows me. Why can't he take a hint? I don't need him in my space, not today.

"You can go."

"Not leaving," he says flatly.

I walk straight to the kitchen and grab a glass and pour some whiskey. I hand it to Xander and then take a swig straight from the bottle. This is not normal for me but after the day I've had, fuck it.

"We found her."

A relieved look is written all over his face. "Is she alright? Does she have injuries?"

"No—I mean yeah, I think physically she'll be okay. We walked in on Nash almost raping her. Two seconds later and we would've been too late. Emotionally, I'm not sure how you recover from something like this. That spark in her eyes was gone."

He pinches the bridge of his nose, "Jesus."

"He had his fucking dick out, half an inch away. I'll never get that shit out of my brain."

He takes a long gulp of his drink. "So where is she now? And why the hell aren't you with her?"

"It's over between us."

Slamming his glass down, he reacts, "Liam, tell me you didn't just break up with her after what she's been through."

I shake my head, "Of course not, dickhead. She ended it. Mercy asked me to leave her alone. After what she's been through because of me, it's the least I can do. I'm letting her go."

"Can you do that?" He asks with a shocked expression.

"Man, I don't have a choice. It's the only thing she asked of me. You should have seen her. I just have to." I take a big gulp of whiskey from the bottle, "I can't be the one to cause her more pain. I will do what she wants even if it fucking kills me, and it just might."

He takes another drink of his whisky, "Why don't you come stay with me and Isabella for a bit?"

"I can't."

"Why can't you?"

I sigh, "I have to be here in case she changes her mind."

"What about work?" he asks.

"I'm taking some time off."

"Liam, seriously. You can't just sit here in this house all by yourself, haunted by memories slowly driving you insane."

Why can't he just leave? I don't want him here; I need to be alone. I don't need him trying to save me from myself. Nobody can save me except Mercy and I already know that isn't going to happen.

"Xander, listen, I know you're trying to help, but I really need to be alone right now."

He glances around, "Who cleaned up? You said the house was trashed."

"My maid."

He nods, "Alright, I'll go for now. But I'll see you soon, yeah?"

Finally, he turns and leaves. I'm all alone with this pain in my chest. A few hours later I get a call from a number I don't recognize but for some reason I answer it.

"Dad. I need a lawyer."

I take a deep breath to control my rage, "Are you fucking kidding me? Abso-fucking-lutely not!"

I hang up.

I did not want him dead. I want him to live with what he did. He's my son, I'll always love him no matter what. But I'm done. I certainly will not help him get out of jail, that's for damn sure. One thing is certain, my son has balls of steel.

Three

LIAM

ONE MONTH LATER...

All charges were dropped against me which I was grateful for, but my world stopped the day I lost Mercy. She never came to pick up any of her things, it's all sitting in my closet right where she left it. I have not called or even sent a text message. She wanted me to let her go and I have. Thanks to the magic of social media, I see that she's okay. She has bounced back while I have not.

Tonight, she's at On-Call, she checked in there on Facebook. Xander texted me and told me I should just casually drop by. But I'm not going to, that would be stalker-like, right? If I'm honest with myself, I couldn't possibly stand to hear those words from her mouth again. *It's over Liam.* It's bad enough that they play on repeat in my fucking head. I don't need to actually hear them again.

I'm no longer the man she wants. I don't think it was anything I did. We were just fine until my asshole son kidnapped her and tried to rape her. Maybe it changed the way she sees me. Who could blame her really? Nash and I do look alike, perhaps she can't stomach looking at me again. It's pretty hard to have a relationship with someone that you can't stand looking at.

A knock at my door snaps me out of my memories that seem to be on a twenty-four/seven torture reel.

I open the door to a police officer.

"Are you Dr. Liam Lexington?"

"Yes, how can I help you?"

"I'm Sergeant Benson, there has been an accident."

I wave her in and immediately I start pacing, "Who?"

Please let Mercy be okay. She's at the On-Call Room I remind myself, she's safe.

"Your parents were hit by a drunk driver going the wrong way on the freeway. I'm sorry, sir, but they didn't make it."

She keeps talking but I don't hear anything else. When she leaves, I call my little sister, Elle, and tell her what happened. After listening to her sob for an hour I book her a flight to come home. My sister is a supermodel, mostly in lingerie which I don't like but at twenty she doesn't listen to me. She's simply stunning with blonde hair to the middle of her back and crystal blue eyes, it's not at all surprising to me that she's done so well for herself. Still, I wish it involved more clothes.

* * *

The Next Morning

As I wait for her flight to arrive, I call Xander to let him know about my parents. He's heartbroken as I knew he would be. He's known my parents for a long time and is closer to them than I think I have ever been.

After I've notified everyone there is to inform, I head out to my car to go to the airport to pick up my baby sister. It's a thirty-five-minute drive and the traffic is surprisingly light. I pull up to the curb to get her and she's standing outside with a man that can only be described as a pillar of stone. She didn't mention a boyfriend, but I already don't like this guy whoever the hell he is.

I get out and open the back of my vehicle for her suitcases, four. She does not travel light. Elle runs up and throws her arms around me the same way she did when she was a little girl. "LIAM!"

I whisper to her, "Who is the guy that looks like he wants to kill me?"

She giggles, "That's Max, he's my security guy. He always looks like that."

I kiss her on the forehead and then release her so I can put her suitcases in the car. She gets in the passenger seat while Stony Max climbs in the back. This man is so huge that he has to sit, slanted to even fit in the car. Where did she find this fucking gorilla?

As we drive, I try to make small talk, "How was the flight?"

"Fine."

Again, she starts to cry, "Is he going to jail?"

"He was arrested but hasn't been charged yet."

She sniffles, "I'm talking about Nash."

I sigh, I know this is hard for her. I hated even telling her about what happened. Nash is really more like a brother to her; they grew up together. My parents who thought they could never have kids adopted me and my brother after trying for five years. Twenty years later in the middle of peri-menopause Elle surprised everyone. Nash was three when she was born, and he instantly loved her.

"Yeah, he's going to jail. Well prison probably. He kidnapped and attempted to rape a woman."

"*Your* woman," she states.

I grip the steering wheel tight, "At the time."

She gapes at me, "What?"

I blink back the tears threatening to fall, "She ended things after Nash..."

I can't even finish the sentence. A month later and it's still so painful and I can only imagine how terrible it has been for Mercy. Then I remind myself that I'm the only one suffering. She seems fine, on social media anyway.

"Oh Liam," she says while tenderly touching my knee, "I'm sorry."

I take a deep breath, "It's fine, but I prefer not to talk about it."

"Maybe she needs time after going through a traumatic experience like that."

"Elle."

"Right, you don't want to talk about it but maybe you need to."

As I pull into the driveway, I glance over at my beautiful sister, "I'm glad you're here. I missed you."

She smiles a huge grin, "I missed you too, Li-Li."

"Don't start that."

When she was little, she couldn't pronounce my name, so she called me Li Li. It was cute then, but it is not cute now.

I grab two of her suitcases while Max grabs the other two, and we walk into the house, and I show Max to her room.

"You can take any of the other guest rooms. Wherever you're comfortable," I tell Max, "Except the princess one. It's reserved."

"What's with the princess room?" Elle asks.

I roll my eyes, "Let's have a drink and I'll tell you about Ivy."

She listens without saying a word as I tell her all about Ivy, the plans we had to become her foster parents and eventually adopt her.

Finally, she says, "Now what?"

I shake my head, "I don't know. I don't want to petition to become her foster home if that's what Mercy is trying to do. I don't want to take her away from Mercy."

She sets her drink down on the coffee table and looks at me with a raised eyebrow, "Well, what does Mercy say about it?"

"We haven't spoken since she asked me to leave her alone."

Shaking her head she says, "You need to talk to her about this little girl. Neither one of you wants her to get lost in the foster care system. You don't have to talk about anything else, but this is important."

I sigh, "You're such a pain in the ass."

She giggles, "Perhaps but you know I'm right. I am after all the smarter sibling."

She laughs again as I roll my eyes, "Maybe you need a mediator of some kind. I could talk to her for you."

"Maybe. But we need to go to bed. We need to make funeral arrangements in the morning."

"I can't believe they're just gone, Liam."

"Me either."

She hugs me and kisses me on the cheek, "I'm glad you're my brother. Goodnight."

"Me too. Goodnight, Elle."

I walk to my bedroom and it's such an empty room without Mercy. I miss her as much as I did the first night I came back alone. Her scent is gone, just like her. Ninety-eight percent of my thoughts are about her. It's a constantly running theme in my brain. Me proposing, her saying yes, giving her pleasure. And it always ends the same, *Leave me alone Liam, it's over.* I'm not sure why I continue to torture myself. But I can't stop thinking about her, maybe I don't really want to. After tossing and turning most of the night, I finally fall asleep.

Four

MERCY

I AM SITTING beside Ivy's bed as she tells me all about the movie she watched last night, *Disney's Moana*. Her eyes are big and expressive as she explains the movie which really doesn't make a whole lot of sense to me probably because she jumps all over the place. One minute she's talking about the end and then she goes back to the beginning. But I love hearing her get so excited. She informs me that Dr. L will be seeing her today. She'll find out if she's done with chemo or needs more. If she doesn't, I need to figure out what I'm doing. I've spent a lot of time thinking about what to do. If Liam wants to adopt her, I don't want to stand in his way. I know how much I hurt him; I don't want to cause him any more pain. I'm not sure I'll ever get his devastated eyes out of my head. When I told him it was over that look nearly killed me. It dominates my thoughts, the look of pure devastation in the eyes of the man I so desperately love. Every time I remember it all the air escapes my lungs as panic sets in. I did that to him. I never wanted it to be over, it's the last thing I ever wanted. But how could he ever look at me the same after seeing what he saw? Me naked, underneath his son, moments from penetration. Seconds really. Whether I wanted it or not, how could he ever be attracted to me, again? He couldn't, so I put us both out of our misery even though it broke my heart.

"Mercy?" Ivy asks.

My lips turn up into a weak smile, "I'm sorry, honey. I have a lot on my mind."

She glances up excitedly looking at the door, "Dr. L!"

I freeze, every muscle in my body tensing as I turn to look. I know I shouldn't, but I can't stop myself. He's got a beautiful blonde with him. My mouth forms an unintentional 'O'. She's *that* beautiful. Bitterness hits me to the core. A month? That's how long it fucking took for him to move on? Obviously, it's serious if he's bringing her to see Ivy. How dare he? It doesn't escape me that she looks even younger than I am. Clearly, he does have a type after all. I grind my teeth as I attempt to control my emotions. I stand and kiss Ivy on the forehead, "I'll be back later to find out how everything is, okay?"

Liam says, "Mercy, you don't have to go."

Glancing up at him, his eyes penetrate my broken heart, "I really do."

I rush out before my tears tell Ivy things; I don't want her to know.

The blonde comes running out after me, "Mercy!"

I keep walking to the parking lot pretending I can't hear her.

She stops me at my car, "Mercy."

I turn to her, "Look I don't mean to be rude, but I don't really want to have a conversation with Liam's new girlfriend."

Her eyes widen as she gapes at me, "Oh God, I could see how you might think that but I'm Elle, Liam's little sister."

Relief floods me and I'm not sure why. After all, it was me that ended things. I can't really expect that he will never date again. That's ridiculous. He's probably had a dozen women in the last month.

"Can I buy you a coffee? I'd like to talk to you about Ivy."

I raise an eyebrow, "Okay."

We walk back into the hospital going to the coffee shop that's dedicated to the cancer floor. After we both get a coffee, we sit at a table in the corner.

I stare at her waiting to find out what she wants. She really is stunning. It makes me feel uncomfortable. I know I'm attractive but she is next level stunning.

"Look, my brother is afraid to talk to you. He agreed to leave you alone and he has. But we need to figure out what's going to happen to Ivy. He hasn't pursued becoming her foster father because he doesn't want to step on your toes. But he needs to know what your plans are."

"I want to foster her, but I didn't want to step on his toes either. I've caused him enough pain."

She raises an eyebrow and then looks down at her coffee, taking a tentative sip.

"Liam's going to be pissed at me, but I don't care. I love my brother and I have to do what's best for him. So, tell me, Mercy, why?"

I shake my head, "Why what?"

I take a sip of my coffee while she continues, "Why did you push him out of your life?"

"Do you know what happened?"

"With Nash?" she questions.

I nod and she replies, "Yeah, I know what happened. And Mercy, I'm really sorry."

I take a deep breath, "How could he ever look at me like he used to? After seeing that?"

I shake my head trying to erase the pain, "It's impossible."

She considers my words before asking, "May I be blunt?"

A small laugh comes out of my mouth, "From everything Liam ever told me about you, I don't think that's even a choice."

She smiles warmly and then says, "He didn't walk in on his son fucking you. You didn't cheat on him. He found his son nearly raping you. I'm not going to say that it hasn't been a difficult thing for Liam to process. But I am going to say that man loves you. I've never seen my brother so broken. And it's not only about what Nash did to you. It's because he's so lost without you. He's in love with you, Mercy. He did what he thought was right. You asked him to leave you alone, so he did. But this is not what he wants."

The silence is deafening after that. I don't know what to say, I'm at a loss for words.

"Do you visit him often?" I ask, "I'm surprised we've never met."

"We have to plan two funerals today. That's the only reason I'm here although I've missed my brother."

"What? Two funerals? Who?"

"Our parents were killed yesterday by a drunk driver."

"Oh my God. I'm sorry. Is Liam, okay?"

"As much as possible." She responds.

She takes another sip of her coffee after wiping a tear from her eyes.

"Is there anything I can do?"

She rolls her eyes at me, "Yeah, you can talk to my brother. This has gone on long enough."

"About Ivy, you mean?"

Placing her cup on the table, she stares at me, "Well, yeah you two need to figure that out. But I mean talk about whatever. Ivy, your relationship, the fucking weather. Whatever. But this silence between the two of you? Enough already. Just talk. He didn't do anything wrong, Mercy. The only thing he has ever done is love you unconditionally. Stop punishing him for Nash's choices."

I nod, "I will. Soon."

She gets up, "I have to go. We have difficult things to do today. Don't let soon turn into weeks or months. Life is short, don't waste it."

"Of course," I say.

Turning back towards me, she says, "I'm sorry for what Nash did. I hope you've been getting some help to deal with it."

I nod, "I am."

She leaves me alone with my thoughts. Could I be wrong about him looking at me the same? Could he bear to touch me sexually without seeing his son? I can't imagine that he could, but his sister seems to think so. Fuck, I miss him. Seeing him today brought so many buried emotions to the surface. I sit at the table staring at my cup of coffee while lost in memories.

"Mercy."

His voice snaps me from my reminiscing.

Glancing up, meeting his gaze, all the air escapes my lungs, I can't move. I can't speak. I just stare at him like an idiot.

He touches my hand, and I know I should take my hand away, but I can't.

"Are you okay?" He asks.

I nod my head and he pulls Elle's vacated chair closer to mine and sits down, watching me as if I'm an animal that's going to flee.

"Fuck. I'm sorry," he says as he pulls his hand away.

"For what?" I ask, but I know it's for touching me, he doesn't want to touch me anymore. My worst fears are confirmed.

"Touching you without consent. I know better, I'm sorry."

I laugh lightly, "It's fine."

He puts his hands on his lap and looks at me with unshed tears.

"Mercy, I'm sorry. I'm so fucking sorry for what he...everything."

I shake my head in disbelief. Does he think I blame him for what Nash did?

"None of it was your fault, Liam. You have nothing to apologize for." We are quiet for the next several minutes before I say, "I'm sorry about your parents."

He places his hands under his thighs, and I raise an eyebrow.

"Keeping my hands to myself," he says.

I go back to staring at my coffee cup, "Liam, if you came here to make sure I'm okay, I am. I am not broken from what he did. Sad, because he was my best friend for so long. But I'm okay. I don't have nightmares anymore. I promise, I'm okay."

He sighs, "That makes one of us."

I gasp, "You have nightmares about what happened?"

He shakes his head, "No. I have nightmares about you telling me to leave you alone. *Liam, it's over*, plays on repeat in my brain."

"I'm sorry, I never wanted to hurt you."

He nods, "Yeah, I know that."

"But I did, anyway."

"Yeah. You did. It's a never-ending raw ache. It won't go away. I'm still trying to figure out how to live without you."

Five

LIAM

SHE REACHES up and puts her warm hand on the side of my face. I close my eyes as I try to memorize her touch in case, I never feel her hands on me again. Somehow, I forgot how good she feels. Her warmth, her love, penetrates through to my soul.

"Liam," she whispers.

"I should go," I say, knowing that if I stay near her, I won't be able to control myself. She asked me to leave her alone. I don't know what she wants now. But I can't push her.

As her hand leaves my face, my skin is cold, feeling the loss of her touch, "Let me know what you want to do about Ivy."

I start to walk away and turn back to her, "Mercy, I love you, I will always love you. But I'm leaving you alone as you requested. Until you take back what you said I will honor that. I want you to be happy, even if that's without me. No pressure. There won't be anybody else, I won't move on. The ball is in your court."

Tears run down her cheeks, I reach up and wipe away the wetness with my thumb, "Fuck, I miss you," I breathe and let out a heavy sigh, "Goodbye, Mercy."

I turn and head out of the hospital to meet Elle in my car.

Fuck! Why is it so hard to walk away from this woman? Without her, I'll be okay, never great, never whole, but I'll be okay.

I get into my vehicle, and Elle stares at me, "Are you okay?"

"No, but I will be. It's just hard seeing her. I had to sit on my fucking hands to prevent myself from touching her. I miss her. It hurts so fucking bad. But you know me, I'll be fine."

"I'm sorry, Liam."

I nod as I drive away.

It hurts almost as bad as the night it happened. How did I let myself fall so deeply in love with her? I knew better. I run a hand through my hair as I drive onto the freeway.

"I didn't want to like her," Elle says.

I laugh, "She's incredible. It's not possible."

"You never told me she was so young. When you told me what Nash did, I couldn't believe you'd be interested in the same woman."

"She's young but she has an old soul," I say, glancing at her. I continue, "She loves hard, really hard. I never had a fucking chance."

"I need to go see him, Liam."

I blow out a long breath, "Can we deal with one difficult moment at a time?"

She nods, "Yeah. We can talk about it later."

Deafening silence surrounds us for the rest of the drive. I pull into the parking lot of Jeffers, Artman, and Young Funeral Home and can't believe this is happening. Both of my parents are gone in the blink of an eye. Somewhere I have biological parents, but poor Elle does not. At a mere twenty years old, both of her parents are dead.

"Are you okay, Cupcake?"

She giggles, "Wow, it's been a long time since you called me that. But yeah, let's do this."

I nod, we get out of the vehicle and walk into the funeral home. We meet with Joe Young, one of the brothers that own the funeral home. He keeps eyeing my sister, and I'm not a fan. I'm well aware that men find her beautiful, but now is not the fucking time.

When Elle takes a seat, I motion for him to join me at the back of the room.

"Keep eyeing my sister like you're a starving man and I'll take my business and my parents elsewhere. Are we understood?"

He puts his hands in his pockets, looking nervous as well he should.

"I'm sorry, sir. No disrespect intended. It won't happen again."

I convinced her this morning to leave Stony Max behind today. But now I'm regretting that decision.

I walk back over to Elle and sit beside her.

"What was that about?"

"I didn't like him looking at you like he has seen you in your underwear."

She shrugs, "Well, big brother, sorry to tell you this but he probably has."

I groan, "Don't remind me, please."

Joe clears his throat as he sits behind his desk, "Your parents have adjoining plots that are already paid for."

I nod, "Okay."

"They did not pre-select anything else, however."

He opens a book of caskets, and I still can't believe this is what I'm doing today. We agree on two that are identical, solid mahogany wood. We move on quickly to the flowers. Elle grips my hand, "Can we do some red roses? Maybe they aren't funeral flowers, but mom loved them so much, Liam."

"Whatever you want, Cupcake. If you want mom to have red roses, she will have red roses."

"How about a spray with lilies, sunflowers, and delphinium for your dad and a red and white rose spray for your mom?"

"Spray?" I ask.

"It's just an arrangement of flowers that will stand near the casket. Dr. Lexington, I know this is difficult, but I need to ask. Do you want two funerals or one?"

I glance at Elle, "What do you want to do?"

She takes a deep breath, "Well, if they died together and are being buried together..."

I nod, "We'll do one funeral for both of them."

"Okay let's discuss music."

Jesus, this shit is overwhelming.

24

"Right."

He hands me a list of recommended songs, "But of course you can pick anything. This covers the most used songs, however."

I hand the list over to Elle. She's going to likely be the one to decide anyway.

My parents were both far more religious than I have ever been or ever will be. They were always trying to get me to go to church. I know we need to choose songs that would've made them happy.

"Amazing Grace," she smiles sweetly, "It was both mom and dad's favorite."

I squeeze her hand, "Okay."

After scheduling everything finally, we are done and drive back to my house.

Elle asks, "Does Xander know?"

"Yeah, I'll text him to let him know when the funeral is."

She glances at me, "Funerals."

I nod, "Right."

Six

LIAM

TWO DAYS LATER…

I stand in front of the burial plots with Elle on my right and Xander on my left. Both of our parents are now dead and buried. There will be no party to celebrate their lives. It goes against what they would have wanted—no celebration of life, only grief.

"Here come the I'm sorrys." Elle says as people line up to see us.

Xander whispers, "Mercy is here."

I glance at the line of people waiting to give their condolences, and sure enough, she's among them, staring at me.

As usual, my chest pounds, and it's hard to get a breath. Does she actually get more beautiful every time I see her or is it my imagination?

When she stands in front of me, I'm unsure how to react. She pulls me into an embrace and kisses my cheek, "I'm sorry, Liam." She moves to Elle, and fuck, her scent lingers, threatening to break me in two. She returns to her seat, and I try to focus on the other people trying to talk to me but have trouble taking my eyes off her. After the last person expresses how sorry they are, I take a deep breath.

"Go talk to her," Elle says.

"I'm not leaving you here. It'll have to wait."

"Damn it, Liam. She didn't come here because she doesn't love you. Go talk to her. Xander and Isabella can give Max and me a ride."

After everyone clears out, I approach her and take a seat beside her.

"Thank you for coming, Mercy. You didn't have to."

She looks up into my eyes, and I quickly avert my gaze. I can't look at her without talking myself into believing I see something that's not there. I need to not get my hopes up. I need to chill the fuck out. My heart is racing uncontrollably.

"I know today isn't the day, Liam, but when you're up to it we need to talk."

She turns to me and wraps her arms around my neck, pulling my chest to hers, "I miss you too, Liam," she whispers in my ear.

I move my hand into her hair and bury my face in her neck, inhaling her addictive scent.

"I don't want to push you, Mercy. I will never do anything you don't want. But I would really like you to have dinner with me tonight."

She pulls her head back and looks up into my eyes while she runs a finger down my chest, "I'll have dinner with you, Liam."

I pull back from her as much as I don't want to.

"Come, I'll walk you to your car."

I take her hand, help her stand, and walk her to the parking lot. When we get to her car, she unlocks the door, turns to me, and...fuck me, she's so beautiful. Her long wavy, dark hair hangs down to her ass. She stares at me with those hazel fuck-me eyes, her bottom lip between her teeth. I want nothing more than to push her against the car and wrap my hand around her throat while I kiss her. But I won't. I will never make the first move. Instead, I stand staring at her pouty lips, as if I can somehow will them to mine.

I force my eyes to hers, away from her luscious lips, "Six o'clock work for you?"

She smiles softly, "Yes, where?"

"My house if that's okay. Shit. We can go somewhere else."

It just clicked in my brain that's where she was kidnapped.

"Your house is fine, Liam. I'm okay."

"If, you're sure. I don't mind making other arrangements. We are just talking; we can do that anywhere."

She rolls her eyes, "Your house is fine, Liam. Don't treat me like I'm made of glass."

"Okay, I'll see you tonight."

I turn to walk away, "Liam!" She yells, her voice cracks, making it sound like a desperate plea.

Looking back at her, she says, "Aren't you even going to kiss me?"

I walk back to her and take her face in my hands, "Is that what you want? You want me to kiss you?"

She nods with heat in her eyes.

I lean forward and kiss her cheek, "Not until we talk." I walk over to my car and get in.

Fuck! I wanted to kiss her so badly it nearly killed me. But I know I need to be very careful. Everything needs to be on her terms. And we must talk. I still don't understand why she said it was over. I need to know what the hell has been going through her beautiful mind.

* * *

I walk into my home and find Xander, Isabella, and Elle talking at the kitchen table. Max stands off to the corner, scrolling on his phone.

"WELL?" Elle yells when I approach them.

"I love you all. But I need you gone by five."

Xander raises an eyebrow, "Mercy?"

I nod, "She's coming over for dinner."

Elle claps excitedly like a little kid. Sometimes, she really reminds me of Ivy.

I laugh, "We're just talking."

Isabella smiles, "Well that's a start."

"Let's go then, let Romeo get ready for tonight," Xander says.

"Romeo?" I ask.

He slaps my back, "Do you prefer Doc Delicious?"

I groan, "I do not."

They all leave, and Xander, who I can always count on for kind words, yells, "Don't fuck this up, asshole."

I shake my head as they leave.

After my shower, wracked by nerves, I whip up a quick dinner.

When have I ever been so nervous about a woman? Never, but I've never been madly in love with one, either. Fuck, I want her with every fiber of my being. I do not want to fuck this up. No, it's not a want, I need her. Every single part of me yearns for her like I might die without her.

Shit! What if I'm completely overthinking things? Maybe she's just coming to talk about Ivy. But she asked me to kiss her. *Fuck*. My head is confused like a teenage girl with her first crush.

I plate the dinner and put it on the table with wine.

At exactly six, my doorbell rings. I wipe my sweaty palms on my black jeans as I walk to open the door.

I stand there speechless as I gaze up and down her body, taking in her curves in the tiny, form-fitting baby pink dress she's wearing. Her tits spill over the top, and I can't think straight.

"Can I come in?"

I shake my head, "Yeah, sorry."

"I made your favorite."

She pours us both a glass of her favorite wine, "The expensive stuff?"

"Anything for you," I state.

She gives me a smile and it threatens to melt me into a puddle. What this woman does to me still confuses me. I've never met anyone like her.

We take a seat at the table across from each other. I watch her intently as she takes a sip of wine. My eyes gravitate to her throat, the way it bobs as she swallows makes my pants snug.

I take a deep breath as she eats a forkful of salmon. I'm waiting for her to speak, but it's making me a little crazy.

She moans from the taste of her food, and I'm close to exploding. I haven't heard my favorite sound in so long. I clear my throat, trying to focus and get my swollen dick in check.

"What did you want to talk about, Mercy?"

She puts her fork down and grips the sides of her chair, "What happened."

"You came here to talk about my son?"

"I don't want to talk about him, Liam, I wanted to talk about what happened after."

I nod, "Good. I definitely have questions about that."

She picks up her wine glass and takes a long gulp. "What are your questions?"

"Can we sit on the couch? This feels weird." She asks.

"We can sit anywhere you want to."

I adjust myself slightly and follow her, and she sits in our corner of the couch where she has fallen asleep in my arms so many times. After she was gone it became a source of comfort. Or was it torture? I'm not sure.

"Why, Mercy? What did I do? I've tried so hard to figure it out, but I can't."

A tear falls down her cheek, "Liam, it was nothing you did."

I take a seat on the other end of the couch, "Then why?"

"I knew after seeing me like that you could never look at me the same again. It's different now. You will never get that image of me out of your head. You won't want to be with me sexually. That night changed everything for us. It could never be the same."

I rub the stubble on my jaw, "That's why I've been tortured with living a life without you?"

"You aren't the only one, Liam."

My head snaps as I stare at her, and she says, "That's been tortured, don't be stupid."

"Did you just call me stupid?"

She grins, "Nope. I said don't be stupid."

"Mercy, that night, while it changed everything between me and my son, changed nothing between you and me. I love you just as much as I did then. I want you just as much as I did then. I don't see you differently."

"But you wouldn't kiss me."

"Jesus Mercy. I said not until we talked. Do you actually think I didn't want to kiss you?"

"Yes," she says as she gazes at her knotted hands.

"I was afraid to push you too far too fast. I am terrified of losing you permanently and I don't trust myself. If I kiss you, Mercy, I may never stop."

"Liam," she breathes, and it makes my cock twitch.

"Get over here."

She comes over to me, and I pull her onto my lap.

I ghost my lips over hers, "Do you want me to kiss you, baby girl?"

"Yes," she whispers.

I lick her bottom lip, and the needy sound she makes travels through my entire body. I tentatively run my hands through her hair and press my lips to hers. She threads her fingers in my hair and deepens our kiss wildly. Turning on my lap, so she straddles me, never removing her lips from mine, she's making me crazy. I'm trying with everything I have not to lose complete control. But she's pushing me to the edge. I groan in pleasure and pain when she moves her mouth to my neck. Of course, her mouth feels amazing. But the pain of losing her and fearing going through it again is too much.

She whispers in my ear, "I need you inside me, Liam. I want you."

"I can't," I say.

Lifting her head, she stares at me, "Why?"

Seven

MERCY

"YOU MIGHT REGRET IT. I don't want to move too fast."

"I know what I want, Liam. Stop treating me like I'm damaged."

He pulls my hair hard, exposing my throat, and runs his tongue up my skin, peppering my chin and jaw with feather-light kisses.

"Nothing could ever change how I feel about you. Nothing," he says.

He hovers his lips over my ear as he whispers, "Mercy." It sounds like a prayer, a plea, and twists my heart.

"Has your doctor cleared you for sex?"

"Yes."

"Has there been anyone else?"

I gasp, "No. Of course not."

He runs his hands along my thighs, presses his face into my neck, and inhales, "God, you smell so fucking good."

Placing his hands under my ass he stands, I wrap my arms and legs around him, and he walks to the bedroom, never taking his eyes from mine.

Setting me on my feet, he reaches behind me, unzips my dress, and pulls it down over my hips, letting it fall to the floor.

"No bra? No panties?"

I bite my lip and shake my head.

"Dirty dirty, fucking girl."

He stares at me while I unbutton his shirt.

"You're so beautiful, baby girl, so beautiful."

I push his shirt over his shoulders, and it falls to the ground.

Standing before me is the most stunning man I've ever laid eyes on. I run my tongue all over his chest and flick his nipple, and he growls.

"On the bed."

I smile sweetly, "Yes, sir."

By the time I get on the bed, he has taken his shoes, socks, and pants off. He blows out a deep breath while he takes his boxers off. He grabs the lube and sets it at the bottom of the bed.

"What's wrong?" I ask as he climbs between my legs.

He shakes his head, "I'm afraid I'm going to wake up any minute and realize this was all a dream."

"Do you dream about me, Dr. Lexington?" I ask cheekily.

"Every fucking night."

He places a hand on the mattress on either side of me and kisses me with a bruising, needy kiss. But it's different from a normal kiss with Liam. It's packed so full of emotion, and it makes my heart race.

I run my hands down his back, feeling every muscle under my fingertips. He moves lower and captures my nipple between his teeth before flicking it frantically with his tongue. I moan his name.

As he moves lower, he says, "Stay with me tonight. Don't leave."

"I'll stay for as long as you want me to," I squeak out as his cock brushes up against my clit.

"I want you to stay forever. I hate sleeping without you. I hate waking up without you. I hate everything without you."

He moves down lower, placing his face between my thighs, and inhales.

"Fuck, I forgot how good you smell."

He plunges his tongue into my pussy, and I gasp.

"Yes!" I yell as I grab the sheets in both of my fists. "Oh my God," I cry.

He pulls his tongue out, "Be a good girl and come for me," then he attacks my clit with his tongue. He flicks it so fast that I nearly black out from the blinding pleasure.

I buck my hips and aggressively put my hands in his hair, "I'm gonna come. Oh God, yes."

He sucks on my clit while he reaches a hand up and pinches my nipple; I come undone.

"Do you still want this?" he asks as he holds the bottle of lubricant.

"Yes, please don't stop. I need you; I need you so much."

He squirts a little bit into his palm and strokes it onto his cock. And shit, if that's not the sexiest thing, I don't know what is. His strokes get faster as he stares into my eyes I think I could come just by watching this.

He places both hands on my hips and slowly glides into me.

Releasing my hips, he moves over me, places a hand on either side of me, and kisses me.

Pulling back from our kiss, he stares into my eyes while he fucks me, slowly moving in and out of me.

"I promise you; I won't break. I can take it."

And just like that, it's as if something switches in him instantly. He moves to his knees, grabbing my hips with a tight grip, and thrusts faster.

"Who owns this pussy?"

"You do. You own all of me," I pant out.

He moves my legs over his shoulders and fucks me even harder.

"So, fucking beautiful like this, your tits bouncing everywhere, so fucking beautiful and mine."

"Yes...Yours," I pant.

I know he needs to hear that I'm his. He needs it like oxygen. I know this about Liam by now. He's possessive and it doesn't bother me in the slightest. I want to be his. I need to be.

He moves my legs off his shoulders, lays me in a semi-prone position, and fucks me relentlessly. This new position hits my G-spot, and I lose my damn mind yelling things that I'm sure are not the least bit coherent.

My orgasm hits me like a Mack truck, furious, without warning, it came in waves.

"Yes, baby girl, fuck yes."

I run my nails down his chest with one hand, "Come for me. Fill me."

He groans as he unloads his seed inside my pussy, coating my walls. He kisses me and then pulls out.

"I'll be right back," he says.

When he comes back, he has a washcloth and cleans me up.

I smile because I love how he always wants to take care of me.

He tosses the washcloth into the hamper behind the door and climbs into bed beside me. I lay my head on his chest, my ear over his heart.

He sighs as he runs his hands through my hair, "I missed this most."

"What?"

"Having you in my arms. I missed you so much, baby girl."

I turn my head and kiss his chest, "I missed you too. I'm sorry, I had some pretty heavy things to work through."

He blows out a long, stressed-out breath, "I have to tell you something, but can you promise not to leave?"

"It's going to upset me?"

"Probably."

I prop my head on my elbow to look at him.

"Tell me."

"I'm going to see Nash tomorrow."

I sit up instantly and turn my back to him, so he doesn't see the instant tears.

"Please don't go." He says with fear evident in his voice.

"I'm not. Although I want to."

I get up and go to the closet and find a pair of shorts and a tank top and get dressed.

I walk towards the dining room with Liam on my heels.

"Right here, Liam. It was right fucking here where he kidnapped me. He fully intended to rape me. But that means nothing to you. Does it? I'm an idiot."

I storm to the princess room and slam the door and lock it.

"Baby girl, of course it means something. The only reason I'm going, is because Elle wants to see him. I can't have her go by herself. I need to be there for her," he shouts through the door.

I open the door and look into his eyes, "I will probably never be okay with him coming for Sunday dinner."

He pulls me into his chest, "I would never expect you to."

Lifting me in his arms, bridal style, he says, "Back to our bed where you belong."

Maybe I didn't have a right to even get upset. He is his son. Could I really expect that he'd never speak to him again? Of course not. But the thought of ever seeing Nash again makes me feel sick.

I lay in his arms and ask, "Does Elle hate me?"

"What? No."

"Because Nash is in jail because of me."

He sighs, "Oh baby girl, Nash is not in jail because of you. Nash is in jail because of his choices, not yours. He has no one to blame but himself. Elle does not hate you. It breaks her heart that he did what he did." He continues, "The reason she wants to go is because of you. She thinks she can talk him into pleading guilty to spare you the ordeal of a trial."

"Do you think he'll listen to her?"

I've thought a lot about the trial and having to go on the stand to tell a whole room full of strangers what he did to me. I don't want to do it. But I won't let him walk free, either. I'm glad my dad didn't kill him, but I want him to pay, just not with his life.

"Elle and Nash grew up more like siblings because they are so close in age. They have an unbreakable bond. If anyone can make him do the right thing it's her. And now, of course, he doesn't have drugs, I'm hopeful that she can get through to him."

I stroke his cheek gently, "I can't go with you, Liam."

A horrified expression crosses his face, "I wouldn't let you if you said you would. You can stay here or go wherever you like, but not there."

"I think I'll go shopping for some things for Ivy."

"We need to officially ask to be her foster parents. She's going to be ready to be discharged soon. She's in remission. That's if you're planning to stay."

"I know. Gloria texted me. I'm not going anywhere."

He beams at me until he sees my expression.

"What is it? Talk to me."

"It's just the sex, I mean it was great, it always is."

"But?"

A tear rolls down my cheek as I blow out a breath, "Don't treat me like I'll break if you're too rough. I'm okay, I promise. I've had about a million hours of therapy. Liam, I don't want you to treat me any different than you did before."

"A million hours?"

"I was in the hospital for a week after it happened."

"Why? Did you have injuries?"

"On a psychiatric hold." I speak quietly.

His jaw immediately tenses, and this is exactly what I was afraid of.

"Liam, don't."

"I wish you hadn't gone through that alone."

Eight

LIAM

SHE STARES INTO MY EYES, "The point is, I'm okay now. I don't want you to treat me like you have to be careful. I want you to manhandle me. I want you to fuck me senseless. I need you to use me for your pleasure. I want things to be like they were before when you weren't afraid."

In one quick movement, I turn us over, so I'm on top of her. Her chest rises and falls rapidly.

Leaning in, I bite her neck, and she whimpers. God, I fucking love that.

"Did I leave you unsatisfied, baby girl?" I bite her ear lobe, tug down, and growl in her ear.

"Liam," she breathes.

"Ah...ah...ah!"

"What's my name, dirty girl?"

"Daddy," she says as relief washes over her.

"Get up. Get naked. And get on your fucking knees," I point to the floor where I want her.

She does as she's told, and I quickly remove my boxers.

"Part your knees, I want to be able to see that perfect pussy."

It takes me a moment to find my bearings. This is the perfect picture of Mercy naked on her knees, thighs parted. She's stunning. I place my fingers on her chin and tilt her head up while I stroke her hair, staring down at her.

"Such a good girl. So beautiful. Fucking exquisite."

Her lips part as she pants lightly.

"Put your hands behind your back, lock your fingers together."

She does, but I can see the questions in her eyes.

"I'm going to fuck your dirty mouth and when I come, you're going to be a good girl and drink every drop, right?"

"Yes, Daddy."

"Such a good little slut."

She moans, and my spine fucking tingles.

"Stick your tongue out."

I lay my cock on her tongue, "Lick."

When she licks the underside of my cock, I become worried that I might come too quickly. Seeing her like this, feeling her tongue sweeping my dick, has me ready to come undone.

"Open, baby girl."

She opens her mouth, "Wider."

I slide into her hot, wet mouth and think I've died and gone to fucking heaven.

Then her cheeks hollow out as she sucks me in, taking my thrusts as I hit the back of her throat.

When she moans around my cock, I lose control. Every thought goes out the window. I grab her head and pull her up and down my cock, fast, as tears fall from her eyes, and she gags on my dick. I won't stop. She said she wanted this.

"Yes, baby girl. FUCK! Your mouth is so good."

She reaches her hand forward to gently stroke my balls, and fuck, I'm done. I hold her face pressed against my pelvis as I come down her tight throat. I let go of her to slide out, but she sucks on my sensitive cock a few more times.

I pull her to her feet and stare at her in wonder.

"Thank you, Daddy."

Did she just fucking thank me for letting her get on her knees and suck my dick? How did I ever live without her? It hits me suddenly. I didn't. I merely existed without her in my life.

I cradle her face in my hands, "Such a good girl. I missed you and your dirty mouth." I lean down and kiss her tenderly because in about two minutes, I will be anything but tender.

I pull back and give her a serious look.

"Lean over the side of the bed, spread your legs, feet on the floor."

She stands there staring at me but doesn't move.

"Oh, baby girl, did you forget? Good girls get rewarded, bad girls get punished, choose wisely."

Still, my bratty girl stands there.

"One."

She crosses her arms over her chest in defiance.

"Two."

"Two what?" She says with a sweet face.

I move inches from her face, "Don't insult my intelligence. You know exactly what's about to happen. Three."

She looks at me through hooded eyes as she still stands in the same spot.

"Four."

Her lips turn into a wicked grin, and then she moves to the bed and does what I told her to do before the counting began.

"Next time you try that shit, it'll be with a belt. Do you understand?"

"Yes."

"Yes what?"

"Yes, sir," she breathes as she trembles.

I run my hands up the back of her legs from her ankles to her hips, "Why are you shaking, baby girl? Are you afraid?"

"No," she whimpers.

I press my cock against her pussy, and she's fucking wet, which I wasn't expecting after a hysterectomy.

"If you're not shaking because you're scared then why? Have you been that ravenous for Daddy's cock that you're trembling with desire?"

"Yes," she squeaks.

"Too bad you've prolonged it."

I hit her right cheek with so much force her feet leave the ground.

"You know the rules, count or I'll start over."

"One!" She cries out.

I rub my cock around her entrance, and she moans. Then I hit her again.

Again, she screams, "Two!"

I hit her again on the other side.

"Three!"

The last one, I hit her simultaneously as I thrust into her and moan loudly, "Did you forget to count?"

"Oh God...No...FOUR...FOUR...FOUR!"

I chuckle, "Good girl."

I grab the back of her neck and hold her down and fuck her, hard.

"You're always beautiful. But there's something about you laying here helpless, taking my cock that makes you even more so."

I pound into her wildly and love how her body lurches forward with every thrust.

Letting go of her neck, I put my hand in her hair, winding it around my fingers, and pull her up, slipping my left arm around her waist as I continue moving in and out of her delicious pussy.

I let go of her hair and wrap my hand around her throat, and she moans so loud I feel it in my own damn body. My mouth is near her ear as I speak in a low, husky tone, "You want rough, baby girl? Daddy can give you rough."

I remove my hand from her throat, "Turn around and wrap your arms around my neck."

She does, and I walk with her up to the wall and press her against it, grabbing her hips, I lift her back onto my cock, her tits bounce everywhere, and it's fucking perfect. A guttural sound escapes her as her pussy clenches down on my dick. She's so lost in her orgasm, tears roll down her face, fuck, she's perfect. We're both breathing harsh, raspy breaths.

I kiss her as my orgasm tears through me like a wildfire.

She cups my face with her small hands and stares into my eyes with so much love. "I love you. I thought I might die without you. I need you."

I pull out of her, move to the bed, and lay beside her. "Did I say something wrong?" She asks.

I kiss her forehead, "Baby girl, sometimes you render me speechless. But rest assured, I feel the same way. I don't want to live a single day without you. Mercy, you're everything to me. I need you. I fucking love you," I sigh, "I never thought feelings this strong were even possible."

She presses her face into my neck and sighs a contented sigh as she throws her leg over mine. This crazy girl, who snuck into my bed in the middle of the night not long ago, has become my reason for existing. I hold her tight as she falls asleep in my arms.

Nine

LIAM

HER PUSSY SWALLOWS MY COCK, her moans bounce off the walls of my bedroom. I start to wake; it must've been a dream. Then I open my eyes to find my gorgeous girl riding me like she can't get enough.

I reach forward and grab both her nipples and pinch as she cries out in pleasure and pain.

Sliding my hands down her sides, I grab her hips and hold her still while I slam into her over and over.

"You look so fucking good riding my cock, baby girl."

And damn, she does. Her long dark hair flowing down her back as her ravenous pussy swallows my dick, her tits bouncing, that look of pure pleasure on her face, her eyes gazing down at me beneath thick lashes. She's perfect.

She leans forward, placing her hands on either side of me, and kisses me while I fuck her. I take all her moans into my mouth as she convulses on top of me. I dig my fingers into her ass, squeezing the flesh as I empty myself inside her cunt. She collapses on top of me. Both of us breathe heavy as we come down from our collective orgasms.

"Baby girl, fuck. You're amazing."

I turn her over and kiss her deeply.

"As much as I'd like to stay in bed with you all day, I need to get ready. I have to pick up Elle shortly."

I kiss her on the forehead and go to the bathroom. I'm not happy to be going to see Nash today for more than one reason. I know it hurts Mercy, and that's the last thing I want to do. The other reason is that I'm so angry with him and it will take a lot to contain my rage. I'm still having a difficult time wrapping my head around the fact that the kid I raised turned into a man that was even capable of kidnapping and raping a woman. I know the only reason he didn't rape her was because he was interrupted. I understand it was the drugs, but I can't believe that this is what the baby I cradled turned into. As much as I don't want to go, I have to be there for Elle. I'm not going to let her see him by herself.

After I'm showered and dressed, I walk to the kitchen expecting to find Mercy there, but she's not, so I walk down the hallway toward the guest bedrooms and find her sitting on Ivy's bed. Her gaze is on the floor, but it's not really. She's far away, lost in her thoughts. I sit beside her and sigh.

"I'm sorry."

After a long minute, she shakes her head, "It's okay."

"Hurting you will never be okay."

A tear rolls down her cheek, "I know you need to go with Elle. I understand. But it doesn't feel good."

She takes a huge breath, "It kind of feels like you're taking his side over mine. Like what happened wasn't that big of a deal."

"Jesus, baby. No. That's not the case at all. He kidnapped you with full intentions of raping you. How the fuck could it not be that big of a deal?"

I pull her into my arms, "I love you. Please don't dwell on this today. The social worker will be here this afternoon at three."

"Will you be here?" She asks.

"Yes, of course. Why don't I call you when we are done? Maybe we can have lunch?"

She nods, and I lean down to kiss her briefly.

"I love you, Liam."

I kiss her neck, "I love you too. Why is it so hard to leave you?"

After standing, I pull out my wallet and hand her my American Express card.

"Go buy Ivy some amazing things."

Ten

LIAM

I PULL up outside of Xander and Isabella's house, where Elle is now staying. She slides in.

"Where's Stony Max?"

She giggles, "I told him to stay back. My big brother can protect me today, I think he misses it."

I smirk, "Hardly."

I spent a great deal of time during her high school years shooing the boys away. They were relentless, they all wanted her. But I wasn't having it. My baby sister wasn't going to be used up by teenage boys with a hard on.

"How did everything go last night?"

I grin, "Perfect."

"You look happier."

She grabs the door handle as we go up and down the hilly landscape.

"Mercy was pretty upset about me going to see Nash."

Glancing at me, she sighs, "She's right Liam. I should be doing this alone."

I grip the steering wheel tight as I turn towards the jail. "That was never going to happen, Elle. Never."

As I turn into the parking lot, she says, "Poor Mercy."

"Yeah, she feels like me going means what Nash did wasn't so horrible in my eyes."

"How did you leave things?" She asks as she steps out of the vehicle.

"We are supposed to have lunch. I was hoping you'd go with us. I'd like my two favorite women to get to know each other."

"I'm still one of your favorites?"

I kiss her forehead, "Always, Cupcake, always."

We left our cell phones in the car since we couldn't bring them in with us anyway. She left her purse as well, bringing only her wallet. We walked into the jail, gave our identification, and filled out a form. A little while later, we are searched and escorted to a room with tables and chairs throughout.

The guard says, "You can sit. He will join you shortly. One hug is permitted at the beginning of the visit, and one is permitted at the end. No other touching."

I nod, and we sit down.

Nash comes in and hugs Elle before he sits down. He looks like Nash, showered and normal. I'm flooded with relief to see that maybe there's a chance for him to straighten his life out. He hangs his head as if he can't look at either one of us.

"I'm sorry, Dad."

I don't know what to say, so I sit with a clenched jaw.

"Nash, look at me," Elle says.

He looks up at her with a tear running down his face.

"Why?"

He shrugs his shoulders, "I wish I knew."

Blowing a big sigh, he continues, "Look, I wanted Mercy for a long time. I've been in love with her for most of my life. When I saw her with Dad something snapped. I know the drugs played a pretty big part. But I'm not looking for an excuse to get out of taking responsibility. I hurt the one person that means the most to me. I nearly became a rapist. I would have if they didn't stop me. That's something I have to learn to live with. I can never make it right."

Elle wipes the tears from her cheeks, "There is one thing you can do."

"What? I'd do anything."

"Take responsibility, Nash. Do the right thing. Plead guilty and spare Mercy from a trial where she will have to relive everything you did to her."

He nods, "You're right. I will change my plea."

He runs his hands through his hair and asks, "How is she? Is she okay?"

"She's fine now," I bite.

"I wish she'd come to see me so I could apologize, but I understand why she won't."

I laugh, "Yeah, that's not happening. You will never see her again."

He nods, "So you're still together then?"

Elle puts her hand on my arm, "Liam."

I nod, "I'm fine, Elle."

"She left me for a month after you kidnapped her. It was the worst month of my entire existence. I thought I might die without her. Yes, we are together. And if I have anything to say about it, we will be, forever. You're going to need to deal with that."

"I'm glad you're both happy. You deserve it."

I'm hit with the memory of him finding us together, and I swallow the lump in my throat. "I never meant to fall in love with her. I never meant to sleep with her either. I tried so hard to stay away from her. I didn't want to hurt you. I'm sorry that I did."

He shakes his head, "I was already on drugs. That wasn't why. It's not your fault."

Reaching into his pocket, he pulls out a piece of paper and hands it to me.

The guard comes over, "Let me see that."

I hand it to him, and he reads it with a raised eyebrow before handing it back to me. "It's fine," he says and walks away.

"Would you give that to Mercy, please?" Nash asks.

"Nash."

"Please. It's an apology. It might help her."

I nod, "Fine."

"You seem better."

"Well, I'm drug free and participating in NA and going to the counseling they offer in the jail. I'm going to get my life straightened out."

Elle beams at him, "That's great Nash."

A voice comes over the loudspeaker: "Visitation is over."

Nash looks up, "Will you come back?"

I shrug, "I don't know. Mercy had a difficult time with me coming today. I will have to see how she feels."

He nods, "Alright, I understand."

But he looks crushed beyond belief.

We stand, and I pull him into my arms, and he breaks down and sobs, "I'm sorry, Dad. I'm so sorry."

"I know, son. I know."

I release him, and Elle hugs him, "I'm proud of you Nash. Keep up the good work. Everyone can find redemption."

We leave, and I have the weight of the world on my shoulders. I hate seeing my son in jail. It's the worst feeling. I know he deserves it after what he did. Still, it leaves me with a crushing pain in my chest. Elle's sobs make it even more unbearable as we slide into the vehicle.

I called Mercy but she said she made lunch at home and could we stay in. So, we head to the house. I'm not sure this is a great idea, considering Elle's mood. But she said she wanted to spend time with Mercy, so I agreed.

Elle has finally ceased crying as I pull into the driveway.

We head inside and damn, my girl gets me every time, so beautiful.

Her long dark hair is pulled into a high ponytail, she's wearing jeans and a t-shirt. Nothing fancy but fuck, she looks perfect. She smiles shyly.

"Hi, Elle. It's good to see you again."

Elle smiles back, "It's good to see you too, Mercy."

Mercy pulls out a chair, "Come sit. I made lunch."

I sit beside her while Elle sits across from me.

"Fajitas! My favorite," Elle squeals. Elle flashes a serious look to Mercy, "Tell me about Ivy."

Mercy beams from ear-to-ear, "Oh my God, she's amazing. She loves princesses more than anything in the world."

I interrupt, "No, I think she loves you more than princesses."

"Maybe," she giggles.

She continues, "Ivy is a normal little girl. She loves getting her nails painted and playing dress up. She hasn't had an easy life but still she's this pure soul so filled with love. If you want, I'll show you her room after we eat."

"I would love that so much."

After we finish eating, Mercy looks at me with pleading eyes, and I can't help but chuckle.

"Yes, baby girl. Go. I've got this."

She jumps up and kisses me on the cheek, goes to the other side of the table, grabs Elle's hand, and pulls her to Ivy's room. I can hear them laughing and carrying on, over everything that Mercy bought for Ivy today. As I clear the dishes off the table and clean the kitchen, I'm overcome with raw emotion. This is more than I'd ever thought I'd have. A crazy young woman set her sights on me and changed my fucking life.

Eleven

MERCY

I WALK UP behind him as he does dishes and wrap my arms around him and he turns around, gazing down at me, pulling me into his arms.

"Everything okay?" I ask when I notice the emotion in his eyes.

He swallows hard, "Perfect."

I lean my face into his chest as he strokes my hair.

"Elle's getting ready to leave. She has a mountain top photo shoot."

He groans, "In her underwear, no doubt."

"Max is here," Elle yells as she runs to the door.

"I'll be back," he says.

He walks Elle to the door and raises an eyebrow at me when she yells, "Text me, Mercy. We'll plan that girl's day after Ivy gets settled."

I wave to her, "I will!"

I hope she gets settled. I have no idea if they'll let us be her foster parents. I'm sick at the thought of her going somewhere else.

I'm finishing cleaning the kitchen, which Liam had started when he comes back.

My back is to him as I clean out the sink. "Well, my sister is kind of in love with you."

I turn so I'm facing him, "Is that so?"

Placing my hands on my hips, I feign a serious expression, "Dr. Lexington perhaps you didn't know but I'm pretty fabulous."

He snickers, "Oh, baby girl, I'm more than well aware of that fact."

"Is that so?" A smirk crawls up my face.

Liam walks slowly to me, his eyes dark, like a hungry animal stalking its prey. He comes around the corner of the kitchen island, and I run around the other side towards the bedroom.

He growls as he comes after me.

I run to the bathroom and hide behind the door, my heart pounding heavily.

"Good girls get rewarded, bad girls get punished, baby girl. I will find you, when I do, you will be punished."

A thrill runs through my entire core as I wait for him to find me. He walks into the bathroom and opens the shower door. As he prepares to walk back out of the bathroom, his dark eyes connect with mine, and he swipes his tongue across his bottom lip. He growls and grabs me, tossing my body over his shoulder. Carrying me into the bedroom, he tosses me on the bed, and undoes my jeans without a word. He yanks them down my legs.

He rubs his nose against my panties and groans.

"Turn over."

I shake my head, and he raises an eyebrow, "Baby girl. Do you want me to get the belt?"

My eyes go wide, and I turn over.

He peels my panties down to my feet and runs his fingers up my legs and to my ass.

"So beautiful. So bad. And mine."

I moan, the anticipation is killing me. I love Liam like this. Of course, I love it when he is sweet and romantic. But when he dominates me, I think I love that even more. There's something very powerful about him, the way he takes me and uses me for his pleasure. It never gets old.

He hits my right ass cheek.

Automatically, I count, "One."

Slap, "Two."

He undoes his belt and pulls his pants down.

He hits me again and then bites my ass. I gasp.

"We don't have long before our appointment, so this is going to be fast."

He grabs my hips holding me off the bed slightly, and slams into me.

"Oh God."

"Fuck yes, baby girl. Come for me."

He keeps pounding into me so hard I see stars. "Daddy! Ahhh," I cry out, probably sounding ridiculous as my orgasm consumes me.

Placing his hand on the back of my neck, he holds me down as he empties himself inside me.

He groans, and it's such a delicious sound.

"Get cleaned up. She'll be here soon."

I stand and turn around, and he kisses me sweetly.

"I love you," he says, pulls up his pants, and walks out of the bedroom. I head to the bathroom to get ready for the meeting with the social worker. I'm out of my mind nervous about this meeting. If we are denied for being Ivy's foster parents, I will be so heartbroken. To say the last year has been difficult would be putting it mildly. Everything has just been hard. The one bright spot has been Liam and Ivy. My happiness requires both of them. And this Melinda Stewart woman from CPS has my heart in her hands.

Once I'm dressed, I sit on the bed, lost in my thoughts, trying to talk myself through what's going to happen.

Liam comes in and sits beside me.

"She's here, baby girl."

He pulls me into his arms and kisses my head. "It's going to be okay, Mercy. I promise."

I sigh as I stand, "Let's get this over with."

Walking into the living room, I find her on the couch with a clipboard. I extend my hand, and she shakes it with a stoic expression, "Hi, I'm Mercy."

She nods, "Melinda Stewart."

We sit down, and I try to get oxygen into my lungs without being too obvious, but I'm nervous.

"Mercy, tell me about yourself."

I nod, "I'm twenty-four, until recently I was a social worker at Pocono Children's Hospital on the cancer ward. I love children. I like to read, I love music, and I guess that's it."

"You're young to be a social worker."

I smile, "I graduated high school early and graduated with my master's degree when I was twenty-three."

She cocks an eyebrow, "That's impressive. But why did you leave if you just graduated? That's a short career."

Liam sits beside me, clutching onto my hand for life. I know this is important to him as well.

"I was diagnosed with cancer and required surgery to remove it. I had a total hysterectomy."

"Do you have cancer now?"

"No, it was contained in my reproductive organs."

"I see. So, what are your plans now?"

I clear my throat, "I was planning to return to work at the hospital. However, if Ivy were to come live with us, I would only be willing to do that part time. She will need some extra care. Ivy has been through a lot. I want to make sure all her needs are taken care of."

She bites, "I'm aware."

"How would you describe your personality?"

"I'm friendly, outgoing, and I love deeply."

"How would you describe your relationship with Dr. Lexington?"

Liam smiles at me.

"Loving, happy, secure, and fun."

"Fun?" She raises an eyebrow at me.

I nod, "Yes, we laugh a lot. Laughter is good for the heart."

"Let's talk about your age difference. There's quite the age gap, correct?"

I sigh, "Yes. Liam is seventeen years older than me."

"I see," she says as she writes something down.

Over the next three hours, she asks a million questions about our families, how we deal with relationship issues and everything else under the sun. She does not seem to like me. Although, she's taken with Liam to an uncomfortable degree. When he answers her questions, she's impressed by everything and giggles like a schoolgirl. I want to punch her in the fucking face. After I show her Ivy's room, she gets ready to leave.

"I'll be in contact, Dr. Lexington."

Yeah, I bet you will be, bitch.

Her eyes travel up and down his body as she stands at the door, saying goodbye to him.

She leaves, and I storm off to the kitchen to get a glass of wine.

"Baby girl? Is everything okay?" Liam asks as he follows after me.

"Perfect," I snap.

"What's wrong?"

I take a gulp of my wine and set it on the island.

"Oh gee, I don't know Dr. Lexington. Is it that we probably aren't going to be Ivy's foster parents? Maybe, it's watching this woman fawn over you like a fucking cat in heat for three hours? Or maybe it's her snarky questions to me? Maybe just maybe it's a combination of all those things."

"You're so accomplished Dr. Lexington. Wow, Dr. Lexington. That's amazing, Dr. Lexington. I'd like your cock in my pussy, Dr. Lexington." I mimic her. But of course, she didn't say the last thing, but she was surely thinking about it.

Liam pushes me up against the counter and stares at me as he swipes his bottom lip with his tongue.

"Baby girl, you have a dirty mouth," he says in his husky sex voice.

"Don't start with your sexy as sin fuckery right now."

He raises an eyebrow, "Sexy as sin fuckery?" His lips turn into a wicked grin, "My girl is jealous."

He places a hand on either side of me, caging me in and leans down, and nips my bottom lip. "There's one thing you don't realize, baby girl."

I tremble under his gaze, he's so hot like this, so dominating. He dominates my body but also my mind.

"There is no one that can turn my head. I'm all in with you. You're my entire world. I love fucking. I think you know that. But I only want to fuck you. Nobody fucks me like you do. Your pussy is perfect. You are perfect. Your insecurities are pointless."

He pushes his hard cock against my stomach.

Dragging his lips up the side of my neck, he whispers in my ear,

"You, baby girl, are so fucking beautiful. It takes my breath away. You take my breath away. Every time I look at you, I fall deeper in love with you."

I moan, his words are so intoxicating.

"Be a good girl and go get ready. We are going out."

I whimper, "I want you, now."

He licks the shell of my ear, "I know. But be a good girl now and do what I say, so you can be Daddy's dirty slut tonight."

Staring down at me, he swipes his bottom lip with his tongue again, and I moan loudly.

"Stop doing that. It makes me fucking crazy."

"Good. I like making you crazy. Go get ready."

"Yes, Daddy."

He steps back, and I walk to the bedroom to get ready.

Twelve

LIAM

I POUR myself a drink while I wait for Mercy to get ready.

"Liam!" She yells.

I take a sip of my drink and put it on the island.

"Coming."

"What is this?"

When I step into the bedroom, I notice she's holding the letter from Nash. Fuck! She's going to think I was hiding it from her.

"Baby girl."

Unshed tears form in her eyes, "Don't."

I blow out a breath, bracing for a huge fight.

"He gave it to me when I saw him. It didn't seem like the right time with Elle here and I meant to give it to you but forgot."

She crosses her arms as she glares at me.

"I think the truth is you didn't want me to read it."

"You're right I didn't," I step closer to her.

She backs away from me, "Don't touch me."

"Mercy."

"I let you control me in the bedroom, Liam, because I happen to like it. But I will not have you controlling every aspect of my life. You had no right to not give me this letter."

I roll my eyes, "Jesus Mercy. Would you stop? I'm not trying to control you. Did I want you to read it? No. Was I hoping you would choose not to? Yes. But was I planning to withhold it from you? No. It's been an emotional day. Please stop this."

"I'm going to read it."

I nod, "Do you want me to leave you alone?"

She shakes her head, "No. It's fine."

I watch her as she sits on the edge of the bed and opens the folded letter.

I'm not sure if it's for her benefit or mine, but she reads it out loud.

Dear Merce,

I'm not even sure how to begin this letter to you. I don't know if you'll ever read it, but I hope you will. I'm sorry. I'm so fucking sorry for what I did to you. There really is no good excuse for kidnapping and nearly raping someone, especially when you claim to love them. I've been in love with you since we were kids. I honestly always thought we'd end up together. As the years went by, you got even more beautiful. After you came back from college, I couldn't believe my eyes. My obsession for you grew leaps and bounds. I wanted you so bad I actually ached for you. Then I started using drugs. The drugs took over the man that I was. I hope you believe that without the drugs I would never have done anything I've done to you. I know my dad has guilt for me finding the two of you the way I did. But if I'm honest, I think it would've happened regardless. I was so far gone by that point I don't think it would've mattered. I can never take back what I've done to you. I will live with it forever. It will haunt me all the days of my life. I love you, and I think I always will. I know you're with my dad now. I wish you both all the happiness in the world. That doesn't mean it's easy, but I'm trying to be an adult. I sincerely hope that one day you will be able to forgive me. My dream is that one day, we will be able to develop a friendship again. But I understand if those two things can never happen for you. I'm sorry, Merce. I hope you're okay.

All My Love,
Nash

Tears run down her face, and I hate this. I hate seeing her in pain. I kneel in front of her and wrap my arms around her waist.

She runs her hand through my hair, "How did he seem?"

I glance up at her, "He seemed like Nash. It's a shame that he had to put you through hell to get there, but he was like the old Nash only, better. Immediately he took responsibility and said he'd change his plea to spare you further pain."

"I don't know if I can ever be friends with him again."

I reach up and wipe the tears from her cheek with my thumb, "Baby girl, I don't think anybody, including Nash, would ever expect you to. Certainly not at this point. At the end of the day, it's your decision. You will never be pressured into it."

She stares at me with a serious expression, "I love you."

"I love you too. If we are going, we need to go but if you aren't up to it, I can cancel."

Smiling at me, she says, "Let's go then."

I stand and hold out my hand for her. She takes it, and we walk out to my Escalade. I open the door for her and gaze at her as I sigh.

"What?" She asks.

"You're so fucking perfect. Inside and out."

"Dr. Lexington, are you flirting with me?"

I chuckle, "Baby girl, if I were flirting with you, I'd tell you that I prefer the inside of you."

She giggles, "Liam, that's not flirting. That's talking dirty."

I raise an eyebrow, "Get in before I show you how dirty I am."

She gets in, and I walk to the other side and drive to where we are going, the On-Call Room.

"Who all is going?"

"Elle, Stony Max, Xander and Isabella."

She giggles, "Why do you call him Stony Max? I think he probably prefers plain old Max."

I shrug, "Because, he looks like fucking stone. I hate that guy."

I turn onto a side street, and she frowns at me, "Why do you hate him? He keeps Elle safe."

Reaching over, I grab her leg, "I don't trust someone that has no expressions. There's no anger or sadness or happiness, just that blank stone-like expression."

"He's paid to look threatening, Liam."

I glance at her before returning my attention to the road in front of me.

"Does my girl have a crush on Stony Max?"

She rolls her eyes and snorts, "No, Liam, I do not. I just think, for Elle, you could be nice to him."

I squeeze her thigh, "If I'm nice, do I get to fuck that sexy ass tonight?"

My cock swells when I see her pull her bottom lip between her teeth.

She breathes, "Yes, Daddy."

Damn, this girl is everything, simply perfection. I love her heart, I love her body, I love that she matches my sexual appetite. Everything about her is exquisite.

We pull into the parking lot, and I park and walk to her side of the car, opening the door for her. I take her hand to help her out, and she gazes at me with hungry eyes.

"Have you ever fucked anyone here?"

I raise an eyebrow, "Of course not."

She winks at me as she hops out of the car.

"You dirty, dirty girl."

I take her hand in mine as we approach the door and walk inside.

Thirteen

MERCY

WE WALK to the table to sit with our friends, and Elle jumps up and hugs me. That was a little unexpected.

"Sit beside me. I mean you're basically my sister."

I giggle and sit beside her after Max moves and lets me in the booth, but then he slides back in beside me. I bite my lip to stifle my laugh because I know quite well, Liam will never allow it. Liam tells Max to move and sits beside me.

I whisper to him, "You said you'd be nice."

"I said I'd be nice, not ridiculous. He's not sitting next to my girl."

Grabbing his face, I pull him down and kiss him on the cheek.

"How was the photo shoot?" I ask Elle.

She buries her face in her hands. "I'm pretty sure there's a cell phone video of me screaming and running in a bra and G-string."

I glance over at her questioningly.

"There were coyotes or wolves. At least ten, maybe more."

I raise an eyebrow as I listen to her story.

"So, they came over to where we were shooting. Sniffing around. So, I ran."

"Umm Elle, I think if you run, it makes it worse. You're not supposed to run."

She throws her hands in the air, almost hitting me, "Why does everyone give me this information AFTER I'm attacked by wolves."

Isabella laughs, "You were not attacked by wolves."

"Was Isabella there?"

"Yes, and she didn't even try to save me," she pouts.

Isabella fumbles with her phone and hands it to me, "Press play."

Elle yells, "I knew it! Some friend you are!"

I press play and watch a video of Elle screaming profanities and running around like a psychopath while a few of the coyotes run over to her. But they were not attacking her. I sit laughing hysterically.

I look over at Elle and smile a huge grin, "They weren't wolves."

Glancing over to my right, I see Liam staring at me intently.

"What?"

He whispers in my ear, "You're beautiful. Especially when you laugh. It's mesmerizing."

Xander holds up his glass in a toast.

"Mercy and Doc Delicious. Who would've thought."

Elle cracks up, "I'm not calling my brother Doc Delicious."

Liam smirks, "Good, one asshole calling me that is quite enough."

Xander and Isabella get up to dance. Elle gets up to go to the bathroom. I know now is my chance.

"Come with me, doctor."

He follows me to the secondary storage room. Since I worked here, I know there's the main storage area and the secondary that only the stock guys go into.

"Where are we going?" He asks.

"Shhh."

I use the code to enter and pull him in behind me.

"Why are we here?"

"Because Dr. Lexington. You're going to fuck me like you own me."

He grabs me by the hair and pulls my head back, exposing my neck where he bites and licks.

"Baby girl, if you get any hotter, I might explode."

I moan, "Daddy, yes."

A growl rumbles through his chest, "Turn around and put your hands on the middle rack."

He yanks my panties down my legs and puts his foot between my feet, "Spread."

I spread my legs as he undoes his pants and lowers them.

"Such a fucking dirty slut." He pulls my hair, "Aren't you?"

"Yes, I'm your dirty slut, Daddy."

He thrusts into me hard and fast, "Fuck, I love this pussy."

Grabbing my hips, he slams into me so forcefully I can barely see straight.

"Fuck yes, baby girl. Fuck, I'm going to come."

"Come for me, Daddy, fill me up. I want to be dripping your cum all night long."

He loses all control and groans so loud; I know if anybody walks by, we'll be busted. But I don't care.

He slaps my ass hard, "Come. Right fucking now."

And I do, I come so hard I nearly fall to the ground, he grabs me around my waist, stabilizing me. He pulls out of me, puts my panties back on before putting himself back together, then turns me around.

"Fuck, you are amazing. I love you," he says and then smashes his lips to mine before I have a chance to respond.

We walk back out to the table, and Xander shakes his head.

"If I could fire you right now, I would."

I kiss him on the cheek, "I love you too, Xander."

We sit back down, and Elle whispers to me, "Gross."

I laugh. "Are you dating anyone?" I ask her.

"It's hard to find someone to date that can handle my job. I don't date other models, so it leaves me limited. Most men could never handle dating me while knowing other men are...you know to my pictures."

"Yeah, Liam would never deal with that well."

She laughs, "He'd tie you up in the basement before he let that happen." Her face goes pale as a ghost. "Oh God, Mercy I'm sorry."

I put my hand on hers, "Elle don't. Please don't treat me differently because of what happened. It's fine. And you're right, he would."

She nods uncomfortably.

And just like that, me and my bullshit, bring the entire atmosphere down. She stares down into her glass of wine.

"We don't have to pretend it never happened; you know. It did happen. And I'm okay."

"You must hate me for wanting a relationship with him," she says.

I shake my head, "I don't even hate him, Elle, so no I don't hate you. I hate what he did. I hate the drugs. I hate that everyone looks at me like a victim now. But I could never hate you."

She laughs lightly, "I don't know how my brother got you. But if he fucks it up, I'm going to be so pissed at him."

Liam leans into me, "I'll be right back, baby girl." He kisses me on the cheek and heads to the bar with Xander.

Isabella slides in beside me.

"Dinner tomorrow. Our house."

I nod and take a sip of wine, "Sounds great. Can I bring anything?"

"Just you and Doc Delicious," she winks.

I laugh, "Someone needs to tell me why you call Liam, Doc Delicious."

They both laugh, and Isabella says, "When he first started at the hospital the nurses were all quite taken with him. They used to slide panties under the on-call room door. It was the nurses that nicknamed him Doc Delicious."

I cover my mouth as I laugh uncontrollably.

"He must've been quite active in the on-call room."

Isabella shakes her head and gives me a serious look, "Nope. Liam hasn't ever made it a habit of fucking nurses. I'm not saying he was an innocent virgin before he met you. But he doesn't fuck around with nurses." She continues, "He's never introduced us to a girl either."

I glance toward the bar, and Liam stands with a drink in his hand, talking to Xander, but staring at me as he swipes his tongue along his bottom lip, a heated look in his stare. This man has the best fuck-me eyes I've ever seen.

Elle drags my attention away, "When is the wedding?"

I glance over at her and shrug, "I don't know. We haven't even talked about it."

I ask Elle, "So Max follows you around everywhere?"

She laughs, "Pretty much. He just stands around waiting for something to happen. It doesn't normally. But sometimes guys will hit on me, and Max will shoo them away."

Isabella gets up and goes to the bar and comes back a few minutes later with three shots of tequila.

We down our shots, and Isabella nearly yells, "Let's dance!"

"You need to tell your husband we need a dance floor," I said as we walked to our little dancing spot.

Gwen Stefani's 'Hollaback Girl' pipes through the bar as we dance like fools singing along. The sweat trickles down the back of my neck. I feel arms around my waist, and I assume it's Liam. I'm spun around so fast I nearly fall. I look up into unfamiliar blue eyes. I try to peel his hands off my hips, but he's gripped me so tight I can't get out of his grasp.

"Hey baby," he says.

"Let me go. I have a fiancé'."

He laughs, "Well, I don't see him here."

Fourteen

LIAM

I'M at the bar having a beer with Xander while watching the girls dance, mainly my girl. The asshole to my right spills his beer all over the bar dragging my attention from the girls as we clean up the mess he made. When I look back at Mercy, some asshole has his hands on her. In an instant, I see fucking red.

I slam my beer down on the bar and storm over to her with Stony Max, and Xander flanked at my sides.

"Get your fucking hands off my girl."

He laughs, "Possession is nine-tenths of the law. It looks like she's with me now."

When he pulls her tight against his dick, I lose my mind. I grab him by the throat and squeeze until he releases her.

"Liam, let him go," Xander says.

Max comes up, "I've got this. I'll get him out. Go take care of your girl."

I look over to Mercy, shaking like a leaf, appearing horrified, so I let go reluctantly and let Max handle the rest.

I walk over to her and pull her into my arms, "Shhh, it's okay baby girl. I'm sorry."

She wraps her arms around my waist, pressing her face into my chest, "I thought it was you."

Holding her tight, I kiss her on the head, "I'm here now, baby girl. He's gone."

"Can we go home?"

"Yes, baby. Anything you want."

We walk to the table so she can get her purse and say goodbye to everyone.

"You're leaving?" Elle whines.

I glare at her, silently telling her to shut up.

"I'll see you tomorrow for dinner," Mercy says.

She hugs Elle and then Isabella, and we go to leave. I turn back towards Max and simply say, "Thank you."

He nods, "Anytime."

She's quiet on the drive home. That asshole really got to her. As much as I hate the thought, it probably made her remember what happened with Nash.

I park and open the door for her. We walk into the house; she kicks off her shoes and puts her purse on the coffee table.

She goes into the bedroom; I assume to get ready for bed. I check my emails quickly on my phone. There isn't anything that requires my immediate attention, so I walk to our bedroom to get ready for bed with my girl.

I walk in to find one of my favorite sights. Mercy, naked, on her knees, waiting for me. She's perfect. But I did not expect her to be in the mood for this.

I reach out and stroke her hair, "There's my good girl."

Glancing up at me with her gorgeous bedroom eyes, she makes my cock swell.

"Tell me why you're on your knees, baby girl."

"For your pleasure, sir."

I groan, "You know we don't have to do this tonight."

She gazes up at me, "I need this too, sir. I need you to make me forget."

I brush the hair out of her face, "You'll use your safe word if you need to?"

Mercy leans into my touch as she whispers, "Yes, Daddy."

"Good girl."

I get undressed, never taking my eyes off hers. When her lips part as her arousal gets stronger, I nearly lose it. I still can't believe how much this woman can still turn me on. Her offering herself to me like this for my pleasure is intoxicating. Her eyes travel up and down my body, drinking me in. She licks her lips, her gaze travels back up to my face.

"See something you like, baby girl?"

"Yes, Daddy," she says in nearly a pant.

I flash her a wicked smile, "Stand."

Taking her face in my hands, I kiss her, pouring every ounce of desire I have into one kiss. She kisses me back, her tongue seemingly fighting for dominance with mine. I'll win. I always do.

I pull back and gaze at the most beautiful woman in the world, "Are you going to be a good girl and let me take you any way I want to?"

She nods, "Yes, Daddy."

"Suck my cock, now."

She kneels and takes me in her hand and strokes slowly as she teases the head with her tongue.

"Open your mouth."

I slide between her soft lips. Taking her face in my hands, I hold her still as I fuck her mouth. "You like that don't you. Do you like being my dirty slut?"

She moans around me and then gags.

"Fuck yes, baby girl."

I stare at her while she takes every inch of my cock, "You look so fucking beautiful like this. You make me so fucking proud that you're mine."

She reaches forward and strokes my balls, and I lose my mind, thrusting so fast into her mouth, knowing I'm close. Every muscle in my body tenses as I groan, I come into her beautiful throat. I pull out and watch her swallow me down.

"Fuck, so flawless. On the bed."

She gets up and lays on the bed and fuck she's so delectable I can barely take it.

"Spread...Look at that pretty pink pussy. Make yourself feel good, baby girl. Please yourself for Daddy."

She shakes her head no, "I want you to do it."

I growl, "One."

She doesn't move.

"Baby girl," I warn when she lays there defiantly.

She rolls her eyes at me.

"Three."

A gasp escapes from her mouth, "But you missed two."

"I don't miss anything, bad girl."

It is not lost on me that she's being a brat, because she wants to be spanked. I am more than willing to participate if she wants to play that game. Game on, baby girl.

I stick her fingers in my mouth and suck on them, causing her to moan.

"Show me."

She slides her two fingers up her slit and immediately rubs circles on her clit. I move closer to the bed, her legs on either side of me as I stroke my cock. Her eyes widen, and then she moans.

"I'm going to cum all over you," I say as I stroke faster.

"Do you know why?"

"No," she whispers.

"Because I fucking own you, and I can do whatever I want to you, isn't that right?"

A smile crosses her pouty lips, "Yes, Daddy."

"Good girl. Right now, I want to see my cum all over your perfect body."

She slides her fingers into her pussy and starts fucking herself hard. The sounds of her wet pussy fill the room and drives me crazy.

"Daddy. I need to come."

"Come, you dirty fucking slut."

I watch her come as I shoot all over her stunning body, making splashes on her tits and abdomen.

"So beautiful."

Grabbing her ass, I pull her to the edge of the bed, kneel, diving into my favorite meal. I thrust my tongue inside her wet pussy, and she grabs my hair as she rolls her hips, screaming in pleasure. One might think this is for her pleasure, but it's not. I love the way she tastes, her scent, and how I make her lose control. I circle her clit with my thumb, and she trembles as her back arches. She throws her hands on the bed, fisting the sheets, crying out. It's the fucking sexiest thing in the world. I climb over her with my hands on either side, sticking my tongue out. She sucks all her juice off me. Fuck, I love that. She's dirty, so fucking dirty.

"I can't wait any longer. If I don't fuck you right this second, I might lose my mind."

She moans, "Fuck me, Daddy."

I growl and thrust into her heat. I hold myself with one hand so I can reach up and pinch her nipple the way she likes. I pull out, get off her and stand at the edge of the bed. Yanking her down by her ass, I pull her to the edge with me. I hold her and slam into her. Fuck, I love this position. She screams from the pounding, and her cheeks are flushed, lips parted, tits bouncing.

"Fuck, baby girl." I breathe heavily, "You feel so fucking good."

"Daddy!"

I growl as I fuck her even harder.

Fifteen

MERCY

THIS IS what Liam does to me sexually. He owns me. There's no worrying if he's being too rough. He's as fierce as he wants to be, and I love every minute of it. He pulls out and says, "Get on all fours."

He looks so fucking sexy with a sheen of perspiration on his chest. I don't know what he's doing, but I get on all fours as he wants.

Coming behind me, he sticks his face into my ass, kissing and licking my back hole, before kissing my cheeks and biting me.

"You're being such a good girl. But I owe you a punishment."

I moan in anticipation.

He hits me so hard; I nearly face plant.

"One!"

He slaps me again, and I cry out, "Two!"

"You have a safe word, baby girl."

Again, he hits the same spot. Damn, that stings.

"Three!" I whimper.

"Spread your legs."

He hits me hard on my pussy. I scream, "Four Ow!"

"Maybe next time you'll think before disobeying me."

"Yes, Daddy."

I hear the bottle of lube open, and I'm nervous. We've only done this twice; the last time was when he was angry with me.

"Relax, baby girl."

He inserts a finger and, once he passes the ring of muscle, inserts another.

"Daddy, oh my God. That feels good."

After he puts in a third finger, he circles them around, spreading me, getting me ready for his large size.

I expect to feel him in my ass next, but he thrusts into my pussy. And then the vibration starts.

"What the-"

"Feels good doesn't it, baby girl?"

I fist the sheets underneath me as I come undone by this toy inside me. He thrusts his cock into my ass. "Holy fuck...Omg...Daddy."

I nearly cry from the intense pleasure. It's almost too much to take. But I would never use my safe word from pleasure.

"Face down, hold the toy in place. I'm going to fuck your ass until you fucking scream."

I lay my face down on the bed and reach my one hand back to hold the toy in place while he moves in and out of my ass.

"You are so fucking beautiful. My good girl is perfect. You look so hot with my cock in your ass, baby girl."

I moan, his words are my undoing.

"Daddy yes, fuck me harder, please."

He growls, "I'm so fucking lucky to have you."

Pulling my hair hard, he slams into me.

"Daddy, I'm going to come."

"Yes, dirty slut come for me. Give it all to me."

My orgasm hits in sharp waves. I tremble, he grabs my waist, holding me up, and a guttural scream comes from me, pulling him over the edge with me.

"Fuck, yes. FUCKKKKK!" He yells. He leans forward and kisses my back.

"You're amazing. But we need to shower. You're covered in my cum."

I giggle, "Yes, I am."

After he adjusts the temperature, we step into the shower, he imme-diately washes me clean. He gives me everything I need. Fucking me rough and then taking care of me with gentle hands. He cups my cheeks and kisses me tenderly.

"Do you have any idea how beautiful you are?"

I shake my head.

"When I saw you at the bar that first night, I craved you like you wouldn't fucking believe. You and that God damned cupcake. I didn't dare dream that I'd be lucky enough to call you mine."

A tear rolls down my cheek, "I love you, Liam."

"Baby girl, I love you so fucking much. I need to know when you'll marry me. I'm dying. I need you to be my wife in the worst fucking way."

I smile as I wrap my arms around his waist while the water runs down my back. "I'd like to wait until we know what's going on with Ivy. I would be so happy if she could be our flower girl. But either way when we know for sure about her, we can set a date."

He washes my hair and lets me wash his incredible body. Our shower time has quickly become some of my most cherished moments. When we get out, he dries me off before carrying me to bed and cuddling beside me.

I lay on his chest absentmindedly, running my fingers down his chest.

"Can I ask you something?"

"Yes, babe."

"You were my first, so I don't know. Um...I know you had others, so I'm curious, is it always this good? I don't know why anybody ever leaves the house."

He chuckles, "Most definitely not, baby girl."

"You'd tell me if you weren't satisfied?" I ask.

He pulls me tight against him, "Baby girl, I would tell you. But I promise, I'm more than satisfied. Yes, there were others before you, but never anyone like you. No woman ever matched my sexual appetite. There were only a few that even happened more than once. I was always too rough."

"Wow."

"You were the first I had anal sex with."

I pop my head up and stare at him in shock, "What?"

"Yeah, that first night was the first time for me."

I lay my head back down over his heart, "What made you do that for the first time with me?"

He groans, "I don't know if I want you to know. It's really fucked up."

I kiss his chest, "Please."

"I didn't know you were a virgin. I thought, if I did that it would be too far. I thought you'd leave me alone. I guess, I figured you'd be so turned off by me, you'd never want me again, and I could keep my relationship with my son intact." He blows out a deep breath, "I wanted you so fucking bad. But I didn't want to want you. I knew it was wrong."

"I'm sorry."

I don't even know what to say beyond that. I was aggressive with him, and now I know he didn't want me to be.

"Look at me."

But I don't. I stay exactly where I am.

"Please don't be confused. It was not a request."

I lift my head and look at him.

"Don't do that. I didn't know then what I know now. I didn't know that you'd be the best thing to ever happen to me. You do not get to feel guilty for changing my life for the better. If I had known, I would have fucked you when you came into my office in that damn bikini. Or at the bar. I wouldn't have left without you."

He kisses me slowly as he strokes my back. This man was so sure he couldn't do love, but he does it quite well. He makes me feel cherished.

I lay back in his arms with my face nuzzled into his neck. His scent has become the most peaceful, addictive thing in the world. Falling asleep in Liam's arms every night is everything I want. Except for Ivy. If we get the approval for her to come live with us, my world will be complete.

Sixteen

LIAM

I'M in bed waking up, with Mercy sleeping soundly in my arms, when I hear my cell phone ringing in the living room. I try to get out of bed without waking her while I get the call.

"Dr. Lexington," I answer.

"Dr. Lexington, it's Ms. Stewart. It was such a pleasure meeting you," she purrs.

I roll my eyes. Give me a break, lady. "Likewise," I respond flatly.

"Your application has been approved."

"Oh wow. That's wonderful. Mercy will be over the moon."

"I'm sure," she says, "Would you like to meet me for lunch. There's one form that I need just your signature on. We have hers already."

Oh, cute. Mercy was right about this woman.

"Why don't you meet us at the hospital? I don't have time for lunch, but I'm happy to make time to sign whatever you need."

"Sure, what time?"

I laugh, "Soon. I'm sure as soon as I tell her she'll want to go tell Ivy."

After disconnecting the call, I go wake Mercy.

I brush the hair out of her face and kiss her lips, "Good morning, beautiful."

She stirs and opens her eyes slightly.

I chuckle, "You're so cute when you don't want to wake up."

"Why are you waking me up?"

"I needed to tell you something."

She groans, "It couldn't have waited?"

"Nope," I chuckle.

"Fine. Tell me."

I can't help the ear-to-ear grin on my face.

"Liam!"

"We got approved to be Ivy's foster parents. She's coming home with us today."

She jumps up and off the bed with excitement and covers her mouth as she starts crying.

"Tell me you aren't kidding!" She squeals.

"Baby girl, I may not be the funniest guy around, but I believe I have a better sense of humor than that."

She throws her arms around me and squeezes me tight, "Liam, oh my God. I'm so happy."

I hold her close, "Baby girl, that's all I want."

"Go get dressed. I'll make coffee."

"Where are we going?" She asks as she pulls back to look at me.

"I thought you might want to go tell our Princess that it's time to come home. I need to call Isabella and tell her to set up an extra place tonight," I wink at her and leave her to shower while I start the coffee.

As it's brewing, I call Xander.

"What do you want, asshole? I have surgery in twenty minutes."

"That's a rude way to answer the phone. Let Isabella know that we will be bringing Ivy to dinner tonight."

"Does that mean?"

I chuckle, "It does. We are going to the hospital shortly to bring her home."

"I know Mercy must be happy but are you okay with this? That's going to be a big adjustment."

I grab our cups and pour the coffee, "I just happen to love this kid. But Mercy is so fucking happy. So even if I didn't want her here, I'd deal with it."

"I have to go. I'm happy for you. See you later."

"Alright, bye," I disconnect the call and place Mercy's coffee on the island while I sip my own.

She comes in and picks up her cup, "Thank you."

"You're welcome. I have to go get ready. Give me five minutes."

"Okay," she says.

I go to the bedroom and get ready as fast as humanly possible. I know she won't want to wait. I'm sure my girl is itching to see Ivy.

When I walk back into the kitchen, her back is turned to me. I take a moment and just stare at my beautiful girl, drinking her coffee.

"Are you going to stand there and gawk all day?"

"I might," I said dryly.

She turns to me with a huge grin on her face. It's been hard for her to stay patient with this situation. It's time to give her what she so badly wants.

"Let's go, baby girl. Let's get our Princess."

As we drive to the hospital, she rambles endlessly, "Oh God, what if she doesn't want us to be her foster parents. Maybe she will wish she could go home with her mom. I mean that would be normal even if her mom is an abusive bitch. What if she hates living with us? Oh my-"

"Baby girl, take a breath."

She intakes a breath, and I chuckle.

"She has to go to a foster home. Going home with her mom is not an option. She adores you. I guarantee you, if she could pick her foster home, she would pick you. Relax, babe. It's going to be okay."

I pull into the parking lot and park. Getting out, I go around to her side and open the door. When she gets out, I pull her into my arms, "It's going to be okay, baby girl. You'll see."

We walk into Ivy's room, and she screams, "MERCY!"

I pull up two chairs beside Ivy's bed and motion for Mercy to sit in one. She does, and I take a seat on the other.

"Are you here to watch a movie?" Ivy asks.

Mercy smiles as she shakes her head, "I came to talk to you about your living situation. It's time for you to be released from the hospital. It's time to ring the bell, sweet girl."

Ivy's face falls as a tear rolls down her cheek.

"The social worker said we can be your foster parents."

Her tiny little hand flies to her mouth, a shocked expression on her face. Her eyes dart back and forth between the two of us.

She wraps her arms around Mercy's neck, nearly falling off the bed, as she sobs into her neck.

I swallow the lump in my throat, "What am I? Chopped liver?"

Ivy laughs, I reach for her and pull her onto my lap. She hugs me tight. "Thank you, Dr. L," she cries.

"You can call me Liam."

I stand up, putting her on the floor, "Alright my gorgeous girls. We have a bell to ring."

We walked to the nurse's station, and I signed her release papers as well as the paper left by Ms. Stewart. I'm glad I didn't have to see her because she gets Mercy upset.

Gloria pulls Ivy into a hug, "I'm so glad your cancer free, sweetheart. But boy am I going to miss you."

Mercy smiles as she looks on, "We will visit."

Gloria rounds up all the nurses, and Ivy goes and rings the bell as everyone cheers. It was pretty special when she rang the bell the first time. But this time...there are simply no words to describe the feeling in my chest.

"Let's go home," Mercy says.

We walk out of the hospital, all our lives changed.

Ivy is in the backseat, firing question after question as I drive home.

"Do you live in a house or an apartment?"

"House."

"Do you have a dog?"

"No," I reply.

"Do you have a cat?"

I chuckle, "I do not have any pets."

"Can I play outside?"

"Yes."

"Oh! Are there swings?"

I shake my head, "No, but we can get some."

I look in the rearview mirror to see her huge smile.

"This is just the best day ever," she breathes.

Mercy wipes a tear from her cheek. I squeeze her leg, and she smiles.

We pull into the garage, and Ivy bounces up and down.

When we walk into the house, standing in the hallway, Mercy says, "Let me show you your room."

Ivy gapes at her, "What? I get my own room?"

Mercy giggles, "Where else would you sleep?"

She hugs Mercy, "I've never had my own room."

My eyes meet Mercy's, and we try to hide our surprise.

We all walk to Ivy's princess room, and she lets out the loudest squeal I think I've ever heard.

Mercy has outdone herself with this room. There are large princess decals on the wall. She had to search for the Frozen decals. I didn't think it mattered, but Mercy was insistent that Ivy loves Elsa the most, so she had to find it. I follow Ivy's gaze to the bed with a frozen-themed bedspread, pillowcases, and a life-size Elsa doll on the bed.

Next, her eyes travel to the bookshelf lined with probably hundreds of books. I watch them, and this is a moment I'll hold in my heart until the day I die. My two girls are so happy. It's everything I've ever wanted and didn't even know.

I clear my throat, "I'm going to go make lunch."

Mercy smiles, "Okay. We'll be out in a few minutes."

Seventeen

MERCY

I SIT ON HER BED, watching her go through everything like a kid on Christmas. Oh my God, Christmas. I can't wait. Ivy brings a book from the shelf and hands it to me. "Can we read this?"

I smile, "Of course."

I lay on the bed and lift my arm, "Come here, sweet girl."

She snuggles in the crook of my arm as I read the princess book she grabbed. Ivy listens intently, giggling many times throughout, but then she gets quiet. I look down at her, and she's asleep. I pull her tighter and kiss the top of her head.

Liam stands in the doorway, watching us with a sparkle in his eyes. My gaze focuses on his face. Damn, this man is beautiful. The way he looks at me now makes him even more so.

He comes and sits on the edge of the bed.

"What are you thinking about, doctor?"

His lips turn into a sweet smile, "Happy looks good on you. Let her sleep, come eat lunch."

"I'm fine. I'll eat later."

He raises an eyebrow without another word.

Gently, I move her out of my arms and get up without disturbing her.

We walk to the kitchen, and he says, "Good girl."

I sigh, "Has anyone ever told you that you're incredibly bossy, Dr. Lexington?"

He abruptly pushes me against the wall and puts his hand around my throat, holding me in place, "I know what's best for you, baby girl. Always."

Slamming his lips on mine, he kisses me in a rough, bruising kiss.

"Daddy always knows what you need."

His mouth hovers over my ear, "Tonight, once our princess is in bed for the night, I'm going to fuck you so hard, baby girl. Before I do, I'm going to fuck your disobedient mouth. I think you need a reminder of who owns this dirty little slut."

I intake a sharp breath, as he releases me. This man's words make me wet, every single time.

I sit down at the table to eat the food he made.

He comes up behind me, brushes my hair to the side, kisses my neck, and whispers, "Good girl."

I clench my thighs to control the desire burning through my body.

Sitting across from me, Liam stares at me with a heated gaze. He darts his tongue out and swipes his bottom lip. Fuck. I'm being tortured. I try to ignore him and his over-the- top sexiness as I put a forkful of chicken salad in my mouth.

When I look up, he winks at me.

"What are you doing, Liam?"

"Eye-fucking you, baby girl."

This man has no shame whatsoever.

I roll my eyes, "I think it's called torture."

"Oh, baby girl, I think I need to make some purchases. There's nothing I'd like more than to have you chained up so I could torture you."

I put my fork down and glare at him.

"Who punishes you when you're bad?"

He chuckles, "Am I being bad, baby girl?"

"Yes," I whine.

"Do you want to punish me?" He asks.

"Yes."

"I don't mind letting you switch for a little while. What did you have in mind?"

"Torture," I said dryly and then take a big gulp of my wine.

He pulls his bottom lip between his teeth as he raises an eyebrow.

"I'll try anything once."

Fuck. How is this man so damn sexy? Everything he says makes me weak in the knees. It's bullshit. Nobody should have this effect on any one person.

I finish my wine and get up and clear my dishes.

"I'm going to check on Ivy."

As if she read my mind, she appears in the kitchen.

I get the food Liam made for her, chicken, cheese, strawberries, and carrot sticks.

She sits down and eats the strawberries and cheese. But then she scrunches her face as she stares at the chicken and vegetables.

"Do you not like chicken and carrots?" I ask.

She shakes her head, "Well, I like chicken nuggets."

Liam goes to speak, but I silence him with a look.

"I'll make a deal with you, Ivy. Do you like chocolate chip cookies?"

She gives me a look that says, 'are you stupid'.

"If you eat three bites of chicken and two bites of carrots, then you can help me make and then eat chocolate chip cookies."

"I don't want to eat this," she huffs defiantly.

"That's fine. But that's the deal."

"Fine," she huffs, picking up a piece of chicken and eating it.

She eats exactly three pieces of chicken, and two bites of carrot, no more, no less.

"Happy?" She asks.

This girl is very sassy today. It will be addressed, but not today. This is a big change for her, and I've not forgotten what she has been through. To be hospitalized for cancer treatment, and then your mother leaves one day and doesn't come back, man, that's got to be devastating for a little girl.

"You did very well. I'm proud of you, now let's make cookies!"

We go into the kitchen; I get everything we need and place it on the island.

"Let's wash our hands first." I turn the sink on, and we both wash our hands. Ivy sings her ABCs while washing hers. She is simply too adorable for words.

Liam looks on with an amused expression.

"Can I help you, sir?"

He shakes his head and chuckles, "No. I just didn't know you could cook. You won't burn the house down, will you?"

I place my hands on my hips, feigning annoyance, "I will have you know, Dr. Lexington, I make the best chocolate chip cookies in the entire world."

He winks at me, "I have no doubt that you excel at everything you do. Don't forget, we have to leave at four thirty for dinner with Isabella and Xander."

"Okay, stir this," I say to Ivy.

I walk over to Liam and kiss him gently, "I love you. Go find something to do."

He huffs, "I already found something I want to do." He whispers in my ear, "She's a cock blocker."

I giggle, "Behave."

"Never," he said. "I've got patients to check on."

I go back over to Ivy. She stops stirring and gawks at me.

"What?"

"I knew you were his girlfriend," she says as she begins to stir again.

"Here, let me finish that up, sweet girl."

I stir the dough, "I'm more than his girlfriend you know. We're getting married."

She squeals so loud I expect Liam to run in, thinking something terrible happened. "Oh my God!" She jumps up and down.

I beam at her, "I was hoping you'd be our flower girl."

"Do I get a pretty dress?" She asks with a sparkle in her eyes.

"The prettiest!"

She claps her hands, "I'm so excited!"

I start rolling the dough into balls and placing them on the cookie sheet, she helps but seems bothered by the gooey texture.

"We'll wash our hands in a moment."

I put the cookies in the oven, then walk to the sink and turn the water on. I let her wash hers first, then I wash mine.

"Now what?" She asks.

"We wait thirteen minutes."

I get her an apple juice and put it on the table.

"Sit, let's talk." I sit beside her, "You never had your own bedroom before?"

She shakes her head and looks down, "No."

"Where did you sleep?"

"On the couch."

The timer goes off, and I get the cookies out of the oven. I get two cookies, put them on the plate, and bring them to her. "Let them cool down."

Then I continue our difficult conversation, "And your mom?"

She sighs, "She had a lot of boyfriends. We had one bedroom and that was hers."

She picks up a cookie and takes a bite.

"These are the best cookies!" She squeals.

I smile, "Do you like your bedroom now? If there's anything you want to change-"

"No. I love it. I don't want to change it."

I blow out a deep breath, "Ivy honey, you know you can talk to me about anything, right?"

She smiles at me shyly, "I know, Mercy. You're my best friend."

I swallow past the lump in my throat, "I think you're my best friend too."

"I'm not going to see my mom again, am I?"

I take her little hand in mine, "Sweetheart, I honestly do not have an answer to that. Do you want to see her again?" I ask.

"I don't know. I think I do but then I remember she's mean to me."

Tears run down her face, "I don't want to live with her anymore. I want to stay with you and Dr. L."

I lean over and hug her, "I want that too."

"We are going to have dinner tonight at a friend's house."

"I'm staying here?" She asks seriously.

"What? No! You're coming with us. They are very excited to meet you."

"Who are they?"

I smile, "Xander, you may remember him. He was your doctor when you had that nasty infection. He did your surgery."

She nods, "Dr. Kane."

"That's right, but you can call him Xander now. And his wife Isabella will be there. She's wonderful. You'll love her. Liam's sister, Elle will be there. You've met her too once I think. And Max, her friend."

"No kids?" She asks with a disappointed expression.

I shake my head, "No. Just you. We are the only ones lucky enough to have kids."

She smiles, "Do you remember you told me about adopting?"

I nod.

"I want you to do that."

"Ivy, there is nothing we want more. The plan is to try to adopt you. But it's not just up to us. We won't know for a long time probably."

She smiles, "Okay."

"Can I go play in my room?"

"Of course, honey."

She runs off to her room.

Eighteen

LIAM

I SPENT the afternoon in my office while I gave Ivy and Mercy some alone time. I'm now showered and dressed in Mercy's favorite black jeans and deep red Henley. I walk into the living room to find them all dressed and ready to go.

"You look beautiful, Princess," I say to Ivy, and wink at Mercy.

Ivy giggles, "Thank you Dr...Liam."

I smile at her, "Get your tablet, sweetheart."

She runs back to her bedroom, and I pull my girl into my arms, "You look good enough to eat, baby girl."

I kiss her quickly as Ivy runs back to us.

"Alright gorgeous ladies. Let's go."

We get into the vehicle and start the drive to Xander and Isabella's house. I take Mercy's hand in mine while Ivy plays on her tablet in the backseat. That girl loves her technology.

I blow out a breath, "Nash's sentencing is tomorrow, and I'd like to go."

She nods, "I know."

I glance at her quickly, "You know?"

Averting my gaze, she stares out the window, "I've been asked to read a victim impact statement. I was thinking of asking Elle to come sit with Ivy while I'm gone."

This situation is horrible. Of course, she has every right to read that statement ensuring the man who hurt her gets as much time as possible. As his father, however, it's the last thing I want. Nash is guilty, and I need to let whatever happens, happen. I can't get involved. I will not ask Mercy not to read the statement, I won't hurt her like that.

"I'll go with you."

I turn into Xander's gated community. "I will have to go to work after."

She nods, "I need to go to the school and enroll, Ivy."

I squeeze her hand lightly, "I love you, baby girl."

"I love you too," she smiles.

We pull into Xander's driveway, and Ivy says, "I hope they like me."

I look in the rearview mirror, "Of course, they will like you. You're a wonderful little girl." As I put the car in park, a big smile spreads across her face.

Isabella comes to the door, smiling as always, and holds it open for us.

"Who is this beautiful girl?" She squeals as we all shuffle in.

Mercy pipes up, "Isabella this is Ivy, Ivy can you say hello to Isabella?"

Ivy smiles shyly, "Hello."

I close the door behind me as Isabella says, "I heard you like princesses. Come with me."

We walk through the front of the house to a sitting room. This house is amazing, Xander had it built the way he wanted. When you first come in, there's a foyer, then as you walk to the left, a sitting room, to the right is a large kitchen, and the stairway leads to all the bedrooms, as well as his and Isabella's offices. The sitting room is decorated with modern touches, with two couches and four chairs.

There are several princess toys on the coffee table. I roll my eyes at Isabella.

"Shush!" She says.

"These are for you to play with when you're here, Ivy. I don't want you to get bored."

She immediately goes for the Elsa Barbie and sits down to play with it.

"Thank you," she smiles shyly.

Xander and Elle come in with drinks as we all get comfortable.

Mercy sits beside me, and I put my arm around her as we sip our drinks.

"Elle, do you have plans tomorrow?" Mercy asks.

"I don't. I've taken a temporary leave from work. I'm not sure when or if I'm going back."

I raise my eyebrow at her in question.

"Losing my parents made me realize how important family is."

I swallow the lump in my throat. I love my little sister so much.

"Anyway, what's up?"

Mercy clears her throat, "Tomorrow is Nash's sentencing, and if you weren't going, I was hoping you'd sit with Ivy."

Ivy gets up and goes over to Isabella and sits on the oversized chair with her. I watch in delight as they play with the two Barbies Ivy has.

"I would like to be there, but if you need me."

Isabella says, "Nope. I'll keep her with me. Maybe she can stay the night if she's okay with that."

Mercy says, "I don't know, she just came home."

Isabella smiles, "That's up to you. Either way, I will be happy to sit with her while you go to court."

"Thank you."

Elle asks, "Are you going back to work?"

Mercy replies with a shrug and adds, "Once Ivy starts school, I'd like to go back part time. But I'm not willing to have a babysitter for the evenings, so it depends on if Monica will allow me to work shorter hours. Ivy needs me home."

"What will you do when she's at school?" Isabella asks.

Mercy giggles, "Read. Maybe I'll start working out."

"What do you read?"

Mercy blushes a beautiful shade of red.

Isabella cracks up laughing as she strokes Ivy's hair.

"That's the same genre I write."

"Really?" Mercy asks with a shocked expression.

"I knew you wrote books, but I didn't know what kind."

Xander says, "Although, she's thinking of retiring."

Isabella glares at him with a look of death.

"I am not. *You're* thinking about me retiring."

The tension between them is palpable, and I feel this is an argument they've repeatedly had.

The entire room gets quiet. We all seem to be unsure what's going on or what to say.

Isabella says, "I have a fan that's a little overzealous."

Xander runs his hand through his hair, "He's obsessed."

Mercy says, "He?" As she sits her empty wine glass on the table.

"Men are not my normal readers, but it does happen."

Mercy shakes her head, "Do you write with a pen name?"

Isabella laughs, "If I knew then what I know now, I would have. But no, I write in my real name and my first twelve books have my picture in them."

"I hope you're safe," Mercy says in a whisper.

"That's why we have a state-of-the-art alarm system with cameras throughout the house. Isabella's safety is priority number one for me."

"Are you hungry, honey?" Isabella asks Ivy.

Ivy gazes up at her with complete adoration and nods her head.

"Okay, let's go eat."

We get up and follow Isabella to the dining room, which is completely set for dinner. Ivy sits between Mercy and me, which she complained about. She wanted to sit with Isabella.

"This looks amazing," Mercy says.

I put a little roast, a few potatoes, and some carrots on Ivy's plate for her, wondering if we'll have more issues about the carrots.

But she starts eating as if we haven't fed her all day.

We eat, laugh, and drink, and it's not lost on me how well my girl fits in with my friends. She and my sister got along far better than I expected. It's as if they've been friends forever.

Ivy says to Elle, "Did you know Mercy and Dr. L are getting married?"

Elle acts like she doesn't know, "What? That's so exciting!"

She nods, "I'm going to get a princess dress and be a flower girl."

"When is this happening," Elle asks.

Mercy giggles, "Soon. We will have a date for you soon."

After finishing dinner, Isabella glances at Ivy, "We have a swing set in the backyard if you'd like to play outside. There's a slide too!"

Ivy looks at Mercy, "Can I?"

She smiles down at her, "Of course. Be safe."

Isabella takes her outside through the back door.

I kiss Mercy's neck and whisper in her ear, "You're so beautiful. I can't wait to get my hands on you, baby girl."

Nineteen

MERCY

HIS WORDS CAUSE a tingle to run down my spine.

"Are you ready to go, baby girl?" He speaks low against my ear, husky and drenched with desire.

I nod, completely breathless.

I get up to find Ivy as she sits with Isabella.

"Ready to go, Ivy?"

She pleads with her large expressive eyes before she even speaks.

"Please, can I stay?"

"She'll be okay, Mercy. I promise you."

I sigh, feeling defeated, "Fine. Bedtime no later than eight. You'll be starting school soon which means no more sleeping in." Shaking my head, I hug her, "Be good. I'll see you tomorrow afternoon. But you can call me if you need anything."

She squeezes me tight, "I love you, Mercy. You're the best mom ever."

"I love you too, crazy girl."

She referred to me as her mom, and my heart did some funny thing. It's words I never imagined I'd hear after my reproductive organs were ripped from me.

As I walk to the foyer, I find Liam standing looking ridiculously sexy, "I'm ready."

"What about Ivy?" He asks.

I shrug, "She's staying with Isabella."

We get into the car, and he starts driving with a dark expression on his face.

"I didn't really want her to stay away for the night already."

"I know," he said, "But you made Isabella very happy by allowing her to do so."

"Why?"

He sighs, "Isabella has wanted children for a long time, but it's just never happened for them. There are no young children in her family or Xander's. Isabella spends a lot of time alone, writing. Xander works long hours. This is probably wonderful for her."

"Are you glad that she stayed there?"

"Hmmm, I wouldn't say glad that she'll be away for the night. I am quite fond of Ivy. I like having her around. But I will say, I'm glad there will be no one to hear your screams, baby girl. I intend to take full advantage of the situation." An evil smirk crosses his lips.

"You're a dirty man, Dr. Lexington."

He adjusts himself, "It's a good thing, I have a dirty slut then, isn't it?"

I reach over and stroke his cock through his pants, "Already hard for me, Daddy?"

He intakes a sharp breath, "Always, baby girl. Fucking always."

We pull into the garage, and he exits the vehicle like it's on fire.

As he opens the door, he says, "Go inside, there is an outfit on the bed. Put it on. Wait for me, on your knees."

I nod.

"Excuse me? Is that the appropriate response?" He glares at me. "Yes, sir."

Grabbing my chin with two fingers, he tilts my head up and bites my bottom lip before kissing me in a harsh, almost painful kiss.

"Good girl."

I turn and walk into the house, straight to the bedroom. I glance at the bed, and it's my nurse costume from the On-Call room. I quickly get changed and kneel as he commanded. It's been a long time since

Liam has made me nervous. Tonight, I'm excited but apprehensive. I'm not sure what he has planned.

Liam walks in wearing nothing but his scrub bottoms, and my mouth waters. Holy fuck, he looks hot.

He's holding some sort of a whip-looking thing.

"Do you remember the night at the On-Call Room with the cupcake?"

I giggle, "Yes."

He raises an eyebrow, "You tortured me. You made me want you so fucking bad. Tonight, you will be punished."

I swallow hard, "Yes, sir."

"Stand."

He holds up the whip in his hand.

"This is a flogger. This is what I'll punish you with. You're very lucky it isn't a belt."

He runs it down my chest to my belly button and back up the insides of my thighs.

I can't control it, I shake.

"Are you afraid, baby girl?"

"A little," I admit.

"Good."

His dark gaze travels the length of my body, and back up again as he swipes his bottom lip with his tongue.

"Get on the bed, on all fours, face down."

He bunches my skirt up around my waist.

"No panties," he breathes.

"Spread your legs."

I move my legs apart, and he says, "Good girl."

"When I saw you dressed in this, sucking cream off your fingers, I wanted to fuck you right there in that bar. You did it on purpose, did you not, to fuck with me?"

"Yes," I whimper.

"Fucking dirty slut. Aren't you?"

"Yes," I cry out.

He hits me hard with the flogger, and I flinch.

"Fuck, you're so hot like this, baby girl."

Again, the flogger makes contact with my flesh. It's not unbearable, but it stings.

"I never fucked a nurse. I never wanted to. But when I saw you dressed as this slutty nurse, I fucking wanted you. I thought I was going crazy."

He hits me again in the same spot, and I whimper.

Then he puts it between my legs and rubs my clit with it. I moan loudly. I cry out and collapse when he swings it upwards, hitting my clit hard.

"Get up. NOW!"

I do, and he hits me again.

"I'm sorry, sir, for my behavior."

"What's my name at work, Mercy?"

"Dr. Lexington."

He groans as he slides two fingers up my slit.

"Fuck. Such a juicy cunt." Again, he hits me, and I moan.

"Get up. On your knees. Suck my cock."

I scramble to get off the bed and kneel in front of him on the floor.

"Yes, Dr. Lexington."

He pulls his scrubs down, and his cock springs free.

"No underwear?"

He smirks, "I figured you were a sure thing."

"Oh, I am, Dr. Lexington."

I take his dick in my hand and stroke him while I swirl my tongue around the head. He intakes a sharp breath.

"Oh, baby girl, yes. You're so good."

I lick the underside of his cock from base to tip.

I moan, "Dr. Lexington, you taste so good," as I take him into my mouth.

He groans a deep groan as he slides his hands into my hair.

"Fuck, baby girl. So good. You suck my cock just right."

I love how he watches me when I give him a blow job. He stares at me with wondrous eyes as if I'm the only woman in the world that could make him feel this way.

"Fuck. Yes."

He grabs my head and slams into my throat and comes so hard. His muscles in his abdomen quiver, and his eyes close, overcome with plea-sure, as he groans through his orgasm.

I sit back on my heels after he removes himself from my mouth and lick my lips.

"Dr. Lexington, you're delicious."

He removes his pants quickly.

"Take your skirt off, on the bed on your back."

"Yes, Doctor."

I remove my skirt, he grabs me, pulling me against his chest.

He slides his hands into my hair and pulls, forcing my head back. He gazes at me with wild eyes.

"You are so fucking amazing. Absolutely gorgeous. And that dirty mouth of yours..."

He ghosts his lips over mine and swipes his tongue across my lips. Then he kisses me soft and hard, rough and sweet. His tongue seeks the touch of mine like it's everything he needs. When Liam kisses me, it's with so much desire that it seems like he could die without my kiss, my touch.

I wrap my arms around his neck, his arms around my waist, running his hands all over my ass, touching, squeezing, moaning. This man drives me wild. He pulls back, and his mouth is on my neck, devouring me.

He stares at me with a hungered gaze.

"Take your shirt off before I rip it from your gorgeous body."

I do, then step forward, and run my tongue all over his pecs. I take his nipple into my mouth and alternate between licking, sucking and biting. He groans, his breathing heavy.

"On the bed, baby girl. I need to fuck you."

He walks to the closet, and I know he's getting things to torture me with. I'm probably about to be tied up. And yes, being tied up, unable to touch Liam, is complete torture.

I was right. He has the spreader bar again. I get on the bed, he walks over to me, and restrains my wrists to the spreader bar.

"Last time I didn't get to finish this. This time we won't be inter-rupted, and baby girl, I'm going to fuck you so hard you'll forget the first time."

As he attaches the cuffs of the spreader bar to my ankles, he notices my unease.

"Baby girl, you have a safe word."

I nod, "I'm okay."

"Good girl."

He stares at me wide open as he licks his bottom lip.

"Fuck, look at you. You're like a fucking wet dream."

Grabbing the bar, he moves it, so it's over my breasts, my legs beside my ears, and thrusts into me.

He's so big and deep, I can feel every inch of him.

Placing the bar in my hands, he winks at me, "Hold on, baby girl."

He grabs my hips and pounds into me in a frenzy.

"Fuck yes. Good girl. Take it. You were fucking made for my cock."

My orgasm hits me like a runaway train. A guttural scream erupts from my throat, "DADDY!"

My hands are wrapped around the bar in a death grip, I am panting loudly, as my back arches off the bed.

"Good girl," he says in a husky voice, laced with pleasure.

He pulls out, places his hands on the middle of the bar, and grins at me.

In a sudden movement, he flips me over, so I'm on my stomach.

Wasting no time, he slams into me.

He squeezes my ass with both hands before moving them to my hips. "So beautiful."

"Daddy," I moan.

"Tell me what you need, baby girl."

"Harder," I cry out.

"How did I ever get so lucky?" He says as he slams harder into me.

He grips my hips hard as he fucks me like a wild animal.

When he presses his wet thumb into my back hole, I come undone, screaming like a crazy person.

"Daddy, oh my God. Fuck."

My orgasm consumes me, taking all rational thoughts and words from me, I shake uncontrollably.

"FUCK! Baby girl, I can't hold back when you come like that."

He holds me down by my neck as he empties himself inside me.

Twenty

LIAM

THIS WOMAN IS AMAZING, everything I could ever want. I can't believe I found a woman that matches my sexual appetite to a fucking T. Really, I suppose she found me. I fuck her hard, and she begs me to fuck her harder. So far, there's been nothing that is too much for her. And she's mine. Lucky asshole.

I pull out of her, turn her to her back, and flash her an evil grin.

My eyes travel her body, that pussy bared to me, my cum leaking out, fuck, she's gorgeous like this.

I crouch between her legs and swirl my tongue around her sensitive nub.

"I don't think I can come again," she says in heavy breaths.

"You will come again. Be a good girl, come for Daddy."

I suck her clit between my lips, and she starts thrashing all over the place.

Grabbing her hips, I hold her still as I suck even harder.

"Daddddyyyyy!" She yells in a strangled cry.

She throws her head back, her entire body engulfed in an orgasm. She trembles while crying out, and fuck, this woman gives me so much pleasure with her orgasms alone.

"Good girl."

I undo the straps on her ankles and wrists, tossing the bar onto the floor.

I massage her wrists and ankles, and then she goes to get up. So cute, she thinks I'm done with her.

"Lay back down."

She flashes me a questioning look.

"I'm done with the bar; I am not done with you."

She forms an 'O' with her pretty mouth.

I slide into her, and I'll be somewhat gentle this time, I know she's got to be getting sore.

Placing my hands on either side of her head, I hold myself up, hovering over her, and kiss her while I move in and out in long, deep, slow, strokes.

She wraps her arms around me, her fingers stroking my hair.

I pull back from our kiss breathlessly, "I love you, baby girl. You're so perfect."

"I love you too," she smiles a small smile.

My thrusts are a little faster as she digs her nails into my shoulders.

"Daddy. I'm going to..."

Her pussy clenches my cock like a fucking vise and unexpectedly pulls my orgasm from my body. I groan loudly as I release inside my beautiful girl.

I pull out of her and stand beside the bed. If I lay down for even a moment, I'm done. This has been the most exhausting yet delicious night I've had in a long time.

"Shower then bed, baby girl."

As she walks to the shower, I see my cum running down her legs and fuck me, it's such an erotic sight.

I could easily fuck her again, but I won't. She has had enough for tonight. I turn the shower on and get the temperature the way she likes it. It's a little warm for me, but for her, I'll sacrifice my skin. I step in, and she steps in behind me.

When I wash her hair, she moans, and my body reacts. After I rinse her, she glances down, "Really?"

"I can't help the way my body reacts to you, baby girl."

We both wash off, and I'm ready to get out when she pushes me up against the back wall.

"My pussy is out of commission for the rest of the night, Dr. Lexington. But my mouth is not."

She kneels in front of me and takes my cock into her mouth, no foreplay, just straight to it.

"Mercy," I moan.

She grabs my hips as she moves up and down my dick, moaning the whole time. I fight myself to take control. I want to let her control this. Mercy looked up at me, my cock in her mouth, fuck she's incredible.

She strokes my balls while she sucks me. I'm in a warm, wet heaven.

She bobs her head up and down faster. I try to hold on because I never want this to end, but I can't. She literally rips the orgasm out of me. Our moans fill the air as I come into her throat.

I help her up and rub her knees.

We get out, and I wrap her in a towel after I dry her off. Then I dry off quickly.

"Bed, baby girl."

She yawns, and it's the cutest thing. My girl is spent.

We climb into bed, and she nuzzles up against my chest. As much as I love fucking her, I think I love this more. I'm so fucking gone over this girl. I thought I loved Nash's mom then, but it was never like this. With this sheer intensity, there's nothing I wouldn't do to hold onto this woman–nothing.

"That was incredible," she says sleepily.

"You were incredible, baby girl."

And to think, not long ago, she was concerned that she couldn't keep me satisfied sexually. There's zero chance of that.

I stroke her back as she falls asleep, feeling like the luckiest man in the entire world. After staring at her for the longest time, I finally fell asleep.

* * *

I wake up in my least favorite way to wake up, without Mercy. I get up, pull on a pair of boxers, and look for her. She has made coffee, but she's not in the kitchen. I look in the guest bedrooms and Ivy's. She isn't there either. Fuck, where is she? Panic runs through me. Please tell me she didn't leave me. We are happy, aren't we? Do I focus too much on my needs and miss hers completely? My heart pounds as I make my way down to the gym. She's not there. She's gone. My world tilts off its axis in a moment, and crashes and burns. I've never felt more unstable in my entire life. I went through last night trying to figure out what I did or didn't do but came up empty.

I fetch my phone and text her.

Baby Girl: I don't know why you left. I'm going out of my mind here. I love you. Let me know you're safe, I guess.

I stand with my phone in my hand, staring out the kitchen window facing the backyard.

"Baby, why would you think I left you?"

I turn around as relief fucking floods me. My beautiful girl is standing in front of me, looking radiant in her short white silk robe.

I wrap my arms around her, pulling her tight against me.

"Where were you?" I ask.

"In your office. I was writing my statement for court."

I clutch onto her for dear life as my world tries to right itself.

She lifts her head, gazing at me and touches my cheek tenderly.

"Why, Liam? Why would you think that?"

I shake my head, "I don't know. Maybe, because it's my greatest fear."

I've never been an insecure man, but the thought of losing her makes me insecure, and I do not fucking like it one bit.

"Liam, I have wanted you for a very long time. You. Us. It's everything I've ever wanted and more. I love you. I will never leave you. You give me everything I need. Please do not worry."

I lean down and kiss her with every ounce of passion I feel for her. She pulls back, "We have to get ready to go. We don't have time for your sexual expertise."

"Expertise?" I raise an eyebrow.

She runs her hand down my bare chest, "Oh, Dr. Lexington, you are an expert in all things sexual."

When she turns to walk out of the room, I smack her ass, and she yelps, making me chuckle.

We take separate showers because we both know if I get her in the shower, naked, I'm fucking her. I cannot control myself with her body, naked, wet, and in front of me.

She comes out of the bathroom in a black pencil skirt and a soft pink button-down blouse. I know she's not trying to look sexy for court. But it doesn't matter what she wears, she always looks sexy as hell.

"You look beautiful, baby girl."

"Thank you," she smiles shyly.

I nod, "Ready to go? Do you have your statement?"

"I am and I do."

We head out to the garage, get into my Escalade, and head to the courthouse.

Twenty-One

MERCY

TO SAY I'm a bundle of nerves would be the understatement of the year. I wish I could've done this alone, without Liam here, but I know two things. One, Nash is his son, and of course, he should be here. And two, he'd want to be here for me no matter what. I know this must be a horrible situation for him to be in. His son is being sentenced for crimes against his fiancé'. He hasn't said much to me, but I know it must be tearing him up inside.

"Liam, you know you can leave the courtroom while I read my statement, right?"

He nods, "I'm fine."

"There is no way that can possibly be true. You're in a difficult situation, Liam. I understand that."

He takes my hand and kisses my fingers as we approach the courthouse.

"It's a terrible situation, baby girl. But if I'm forced to take a side, it's yours. What my son did to you is disgusting. He needs to pay for his crimes. I'm just grateful that you're okay."

I blow out a deep breath as we pull into the parking lot. This is the last thing I want to do today, but I must. Nash is being sentenced for kidnapping and assault. They had originally charged him with rape, but luckily, he did not rape me. He came closer than I liked, but I was spared, barely.

Liam parks and sits quietly for a few minutes before speaking.

"I want you to know, Mercy, no matter what you say in there, I will not be upset or angry. You are entitled to say whatever you feel. I do not want you to not speak your heart and mind, because of me."

I nod, "I know, Liam. Thank you."

We get out of the car and go into the courthouse. After what seems like an eternity, we get through security and go to courtroom A17, where Nash's life will change forever.

Nash is brought in, and he spots Liam and then me, he hangs his head. He looks like he hasn't slept in a week. It breaks my heart that it came to this for him to get off the drugs. I just want to go back in time and for it all to be different. I don't want to be here to watch my former best friend be sentenced for kidnapping me. How did this happen? We are all told to stand, and the judge enters.

The prosecution gets up and highlights what he did to me and the fact that he plead guilty. He's asking for the maximum sentence.

His defense attorney gets up next and speaks to the court. His version is a little different. Without the drugs, he would never have committed these crimes. And he mentions that he plead guilty to prevent me from having to testify. Next, he talks about a session with a psychiatrist, in which the doctor said he was unlikely to reoffend if he could abstain from drugs. He is pretty good for a legal aid lawyer. Liam refused to pay for a lawyer, given the circumstances. I never agreed or disagreed with that choice. It was Liam's choice, not mine.

The judge asks, "Do we have a Victim Impact Statement today?"

The prosecuting attorney stands, "Yes, your honor."

"We will hear that now."

The attorney comes to get me, and I'm taken to the podium set up for me to read my statement.

I clear my throat as I prepare to read my prepared paper.

"Nash and I had been best friends since we were five years old. I know the man he was and the man he became after he started using drugs. They are not the same person. It was the worst thing in the world to me when he kidnapped me. The fact

that my best friend could hurt me in such a way was confusing at best. It's not a day I will soon forget. I spent a week in the hospital afterward on a psychiatric hold. I was deemed a threat to myself at the time. I wasn't suicidal, but I couldn't eat, sleep, or stop crying. I had been hurt worse than I ever had been before. After a lot of counseling sessions, I'm okay.

I know it would make sense to anybody here today that I would want Nash to get the maximum penalty allowed by law. But it's just not the case. While I do not believe he should be released without consequences, I am asking, your honor for you to consider a lighter sentence. I wholeheartedly believe he would never have hurt me if it weren't for the drugs. If I had my say, he'd get some time, far less than the maximum, with court-mandated therapy. My wish is that Nash get out and create a life for himself. I do not wish for this to be the end of his story. He has the capability of being a good upstanding citizen. I know the boy I've known for decades is still there. The monster that the drugs created will go away if he chooses not to use again. Thank you for letting me speak today, your honor."

I walk back to my seat, glancing at Liam's shocked expression. I take a seat. He takes my hand in his and intertwines his fingers with mine.

The judge glances at the prosecutor with a questioning look.

"Well, that was unexpected," he says.

"Ms. Madison, I'm sure you're aware that the decision of sentencing Nash Lexington, rests solely on me, as a judge. However, I will consider your words. I do not take them lightly and neither should Mr. Lexington. We'll have a short recess and reconvene at eleven thirty at which time I will announce my decision."

"Do you want to go somewhere?"

I shake my head, "No, I'll stay here."

Nash glances back at me with sadness in his eyes. I know he regrets what he did. But I'm not sure I can ever return to a friendship with him. How do you forget something like that?

His lawyer speaks to him, and he turns around.

A man dressed like a security guard comes up to me. "Judge Hawthorne would like to see you in his chambers."

I stand, and so does Liam, but the man says, "I'm sorry, sir. Only Ms. Madison."

I glance at Liam, "I'll be okay."

We walk back to the judge's chambers, which is simply a fancy word for the judge's office.

Judge Hawthorne motions to the chair, "Have a seat, please."

I say, "Yes, your honor," as I sit down.

"No need to be formal dear. We're just going to chat for a moment in private. I have questions I did not want to ask you in open court."

I nod.

"I've read all of the reports, and from what I understand you're in a relationship with the defendant's father?"

"Yes."

"I don't mean to delve into your personal life but is it serious?"

I blow out a breath, "Yes. We are engaged."

"Have you considered when Mr. Lexington is released, you may have to see him because of his father?"

"I have."

"In asking for a shorter sentence, that would happen sooner, rather than later."

I clasp my hands together, trying to appear strong, but I am incredibly nervous.

"Regardless, I don't think he should get the maximum sentence. Liam and I will deal with whatever comes our way. When Nash gets out, we will handle it. But I don't think it's in the best interest of anyone for him to serve a lengthy prison term. If he was a danger to society, I would feel differently. I don't believe he is if he stays off drugs."

"Thank you for your candor, Ms. Madison."

I nod, "Thank you," and then leave to go back to the courtroom.

I walk back out and see Elle sitting on Liam's other side. I give her a small wave as I sit back down beside Liam.

"You know, if he gets a lighter sentence, your dad is going to be pissed at you."

I laugh, "I know, but he's always pissed about something anyway."

"If you know anything about me, Liam, it's that I do the right thing regardless of the cost."

He moves closer and whispers in my ear, "Like climbing into my bed, baby girl?"

A shiver runs through my core.

I glance over at him, "I have no regrets about that. I got everything I ever wanted, all because of that decision."

"Me too," he breathes.

We are told to rise again. I do, as I take a deep breath.

The judge tells us to take a seat.

"I do not make this decision lightly today. I considered the facts of this case, as well as the victim statement."

He takes a moment and fumbles through the papers in his hands.

"Mr. Lexington, please stand."

Nash stands. His fate is in Judge Hawthorne's hands.

"The crime you committed against your best friend is disgusting. Even with drugs, it's beyond me how you could do such a thing. While I believe you are remorseful for your actions, that does not take away what you have done. Victims do not sentence criminals, judges do. And make no mistake Mr. Lexington, you are a criminal. You preyed on not just an innocent woman, one you called your friend, your best friend."

He shakes his head with disgust.

"I'm going to extend the same compassion that Ms. Madison has shown you today. As you are a first-time offender, I am sentencing you to seven years in state prison. You will also attend court mandated drug counseling. I'm not assessing a fine, because I have a suspicion that it would create more hardship for your family than it would you."

Twenty-Two

MERCY

WE WALK OUT of the courtroom, hand in hand, with Elle walking on Liam's other side. Relief washes over me, it's over. I did the right thing. Nash isn't a hardened criminal. I hope he takes this second chance and uses it well. Seven years is still long, although I know he will serve less time with good behavior. Elle walks with us to Liam's vehicle.

"Mercy, can I have a minute?"

I nod.

"I don't know why you did that. No one would have blamed you for begging the court to sentence him to the maximum. I know you didn't do it for me. But thank you. Thank you for giving him a chance."

I give her a small smile, "I did it because it was the right thing to do. I don't think we'll ever be friends again. But I don't want him to rot away in prison because he made bad choices. If I thought he would do something like this again, I would have asked for the maximum. But I know, if he stays clean, he can have a good life. I want that for him."

A tear runs down her face, "You're a much better person than I am, Mercy. Your heart is simply amazing. I'm glad you're with my brother."

She pulls me in for a big hug.

Next, she hugs Liam, "I love you Li Li," she says.

He shakes his head, "I love you too, Cupcake."

She runs to her car, and we both laugh. We get in the car and go home since I need a car to go to the school to enroll Ivy and pick her up from Isabella's.

When we walk inside, Liam lifts me over his shoulder, causing me to squeal.

"What are you doing?" I giggle.

He tosses me on the bed, "I need a quickie before I can go to work."

I raise an eyebrow at him, "Dr. Lexington, do you even know how to have a quickie?"

Feigning an innocent expression, he says, "That's your fault. You're the one with the addictive super cunt."

"Super cunt?" I giggle.

He hikes my skirt over my hips, "Oh yes, baby girl, your pussy has magical powers."

Pulling my panties to the side, he inserts two fingers.

He quickly pulls his fingers out, undoes his pants, and pulls them down to his knees. Then he yanks me to the edge of the bed, pulls my panties to the side again, and thrusts into me.

He groans, "Fucking magical, baby girl."

Grabbing my hips, he thrusts hard and fast.

"Mercy! Fuck! You feel so good." He keeps thrusting in and out, "Come. Now."

He rubs my clit as he continues fucking me, and that's it. I'm lost to my orgasm. My back arches as I clench down on his cock, pulling him right along with me. He groans as he fills me completely.

"Fuck, baby girl. I can't get enough of you. It's never enough."

He kisses me quickly, "I've got to take a shower."

Stripping down naked, he walks to the bathroom. Of course, I watched his ass the entire time until he was out of my view.

I should let him shower in peace, but the bad girl in me is dying to get out.

The evil grin on my face cannot be contained, as I get undressed. I walk into the bathroom, open the shower door, and step in beside Liam.

"Baby girl." He raises an eyebrow, "I need to get to work. You need to get to the school to enroll Ivy."

I smile.

"What are you doing?"

"Conserving water?" I ask.

"Try again," he says.

I run my hands down his slick sides, "Being bad, Daddy."

He growls and pushes me against the shower wall.

"If only I had time to punish my dirty slut."

"Spread your legs," he commands.

He bends down, wraps his forearms around my thighs, and lifts me, spearing me with his huge cock, causing me to cry out in both agony and pleasure.

His hands are on my ass, and he moves me up and down his length.

"You make me want to retire and do nothing other than fuck you senseless day after day."

I wrap my arms around his neck.

"Daddy, YES!"

This position is such a turn on. He's so strong, so powerful, dripping with sexiness.

I bury my head in his neck as I come in waves, nearly passing out from the intensity.

He's not far behind me, a few more thrusts, and he groans through his orgasm, telling me how beautiful I am. I'll let you know, that does not get old. He sets me down, "Now we need to get clean, dirty girl."

I laugh, "Yes, sir."

He raises an eyebrow, "Bad girls get punished. It's a pity I don't have time now, but I will tonight, baby girl."

I bite my lip to hide my smile. Mission accomplished.

We finish in the shower, step out, and dry off. He snaps his towel on my ass as I turn to the door.

"OW!" I yelp.

"That's a preview."

As I walk to the bedroom to get dressed, I laugh, "You're going to beat me with towels?"

"Maybe my belt," he says dryly as he starts getting dressed.

"I don't think that's something I can consent to."

I button up my shirt, and he says, "Okay."

As I fix my skirt, "Okay? Seriously, Liam? Okay? That's all you have to say?"

"Baby girl if you don't want to do something we don't do it. It's simple. I have your consent, or I don't do it. That's how this works so well between us. You trust me because you know I respect your boundaries."

I want to give in to every one of his kinks. But a belt? That may be too much, even for me. I don't mind being spanked, in fact, I like it, I crave it.

I'm lost in my thoughts when he comes up to me and tilts my chin with his thumb and forefinger.

"Baby girl, stop. It's okay. You give me more than enough, please don't overthink this. A belt is not required to spank your sexy ass. Besides, I'd never want to actually hurt you, so it's better that we keep to what we've tried. I love you." He leans down and kisses me. "I really do need to go, baby girl. I'll see you tonight."

I nod, "I love you too, Liam."

He winks at me and leaves.

I hear the front door close, and I smile as I go to fix my hair.

I can't stifle my silly grin as I finish getting ready.

I'm enrolling Ivy in school. One more step in making her life a normal one. Once I'm ready, I get the keys to the car and my purse. I stop in the kitchen and see an envelope on the refrigerator with my name.

I open it, and it's from Liam.

Dear Mercy,

Please start thinking about dates for our wedding. I need you to be my wife like you wouldn't believe. I hope you'll make this old man's dream come true. Sooner rather than later.

Always,

Liam

This man. I'm afraid this stupid grin will be permanently attached to my face, all because of him. As I drive to the school, I realize I'm happy, really fucking happy. Every day is better than the previous. I pull into the parking lot, put the car in park, and fetch my cell phone.

Me: Six weeks.

Daddy: You'll marry me in six weeks? I hope I do not misunderstand the meaning of six weeks.

Me: I'll marry you in six weeks. I need time to find a dress.

Daddy: Fuck, baby girl, I'm so happy. Thank you. I have an 🪶 for your 🐱 tonight.

I burst out into a fit of laughter. Liam has discovered emojis. God save us all.

Twenty-Three

MERCY

I WALK INTO THE SCHOOL, trying to control the smile on my face. I meet with the principal, the school resource officer, and the lady who will be Ivy's teacher, whom I adore. Ms. Weiss and I will get along famously. Five minutes into talking to her, and I already know that. She thinks I've hung the moon because I am her foster mother and planning to adopt her.

"Choosing a child that has no other choices is admirable," she says.

I smile, "When you meet Ivy, I think you'll realize I had no choice."

She beams at me, "I hope you're going to volunteer to help out in the classroom. You're lovely."

I giggle, "Of course I will."

"When will she start?"

I smile, "Tomorrow but please be prepared for challenges, she has been through a lot. She's had cancer and chemo twice in her short life. There's been a lot of abuse and neglect. Surprisingly, she's a well-adjusted little girl considering the obstacles, but I would expect some issues to arise."

She shakes her head, "Poor girl." A questioning expression crosses her face. "I may be completely out of line here. So, please forgive me if I completely cross it. Are you planning to adopt other children?"

I nod, "We are. I had a hysterectomy not so long ago so it's the only way we can have a family beyond Ivy. However, I had some eggs frozen so we're really hoping to find a surrogate."

"My brother teaches high school and has a student that's five months pregnant. She's trying to privately find a family to adopt her baby."

"I'd have to talk to my fiancé' first, and I couldn't adopt another baby before we adopt Ivy. I can't do anything that makes her feel less important. She has to be our first child."

"That's truly beautiful that you've considered her feelings."

I laugh, "Her feelings are very important."

"Let me know if you decide you want to meet her."

"I will. Thank you."

We shake hands, and I turn to leave when she says, "I look forward to meeting Ivy tomorrow."

I smile over my shoulder, "She's going to be very excited. I already bought her princess backpack. You'll soon understand her princess obsession as well as I do."

She laughs, but it's true. I already know it.

I head out of the building to my car to pick Ivy up from Isabella's. I am sure she's had the time of her life, but I'm excited to see her. I missed her tremendously.

I roll down my window as I pull into the security gate.

"Can I help you?"

"I'm here to see Xander and Isabella Kane."

"You're not authorized. Pull around in front of the gate to exit. Have a good day."

I glare at him, "You need to call Isabella to get authorization. My daughter is here, and I will not be leaving without her."

He huffs and goes inside his guard shack.

My daughter. I have a daughter. Okay, a foster daughter, but soon, we will make it permanent, I hope.

He glares at me, "Go ahead."

Once the gates open, I drive through as I mutter to myself, "Dick."

I pull into Xander and Isabella's driveway, noticing the police car parked on the street at their neighbor's house. I get out and walk up to their door. Man, their home is stunning. There are flowers everywhere. I hope Ivy got a chance to spend some time outside today. I knock on the door, and Xander opens it, "Come in."

"Ivy's in the bedroom playing. I didn't want her around this," He points in the direction of two police officers talking to Isabella.

"What the hell is going on, Xander?"

"Isabella's stalker sent her flowers."

He runs his hand through his hair.

"They won't do anything. It's not illegal to send flowers. This is fucking stalking."

I rub his back, "Does she have a restraining order?"

He shakes his head, "No. He hasn't done anything violent, so the cops aren't helpful."

"Do you mind if I-?"

He throws his hands in the air, "Feel free. I'm not getting anywhere."

"Excuse me, officers."

Isabella and the officers turn to me at the same time.

"I'm a family friend. My name is Mercy Madison. I'm a social worker and I know a fair bit about stalking. How do my friends go about getting a restraining order rather than waiting until things become violent?"

The shorter, balding officer says, "With all due respect, we normally get a restraining order after there's a threatening action. Sending someone flowers is not exactly threatening. So, apparently you don't know as much about stalking as you thought."

"Very well, perhaps I don't. What I do know is that when I ask you for your name and badge number, you have no choice but to give that to me."

He raises an eyebrow at me.

"Please. Do not waste my time. I am asking for it now."

The taller officer takes his notebook and pen out and writes down the information. He tears the sheet off and hands it to me, "Here. It won't change a damn thing."

I wink at him, "I bet you're wrong."

Glancing at Isabella, I ask, "Where's Elle?"

"In the bedroom with Ivy."

"When I leave, ask her to bring Ivy back to our house please. I have a police matter to attend to."

Isabella smiles at me, "Thank you."

I nod and turn to leave, fuming so much I think they might see smoke coming from my ears.

I head straight to the police station.

Standing at reception, I wait since the officer manning the desk is on the phone, ordering food.

She hangs up, "Sorry about that. How can I help you?"

"I'm here to see, "Jack Dobson, the Chief of Police."

An amused expression crosses her face, "Do you have an appointment?"

I stand up straighter, trying to look intimidating, although I know I don't.

"Could you let him know Mercy Madison, Gilbert Madison's daughter is here to see him. We'll leave that choice up to him."

"Sure," she says with a sarcastic tone.

I'm not worried. I know very well he'll be willing to see me. My dad's name carries quite a bit of weight. Chief Dobson started the force in New York with my dad. I know his entire family. Besides, if he refused to see me, my next step would be to get my dad involved. But I don't think it will come to that.

He comes out of his office with the police officer.

"Mercy Madison. My God I don't think I've seen you since you were twelve. You have become quite the beauty."

I giggle, "Thank you, Jackie." I flash a sarcastic smile to the officer.

"Come to my office."

I nod and follow him, taking a seat in front of his desk.

"What brings you here today?"

"I have a friend that has a stalker. Your officer's refuse to help her get a restraining order until he turns violent. I want her to be protected. Also, I think their piss poor attitude could be addressed."

He raises an eyebrow as I tell him everything the officers say.

I hand him the paper with the names and badge numbers of the officers at Isabella's house today.

"You do know that a restraining order will not necessarily protect her? It just makes it more serious for the offender if he continues to harass her."

"I know it may not deter him. But it's the only thing that can be done. It's a simple thing that requires little work. When an officer acts like this, it only makes a victim feel more powerless. This is exactly why women don't report crimes. Because often the men in charge victimize them all over again."

He smiles, "Then let's give your friend a little power back. Can you write down her information for me? I'll arrange for it. Also, I will talk to my officers about their behavior."

I hand him the paper with Isabella's information.

"Thank you, Jackie. You're the best. I appreciate your help and I know Isabella and Xander will too."

I shake his hand and head out to my car, ignoring the officer at the front desk. She pissed me off.

"Call Isabella," I tell the car, and it dials her number. Isn't technology just fantastic?

"Hello?"

"Hey babe, it's Mercy."

"Hi."

She sounds so sad.

"The chief of police will be in contact, and you will go before a judge to get a restraining order."

She gasps loudly, "What?"

"Do I really have to repeat all that?"

A laugh comes over the phone, "No, I just can't believe it. Xander will be so happy. He's driving me crazy."

"I'm glad I could help. But don't let your guard down. There's no guarantee that this will deter him. It simply means harsher penalties if he doesn't leave you alone."

She sighs audibly, "Thank you, Mercy."

"You're welcome. I'm glad I was able to help. Hey Iz, will you be a bridesmaid?"

"What? Oh my God. Obviously, yes!"

"Yay! I'm so happy. I need to go dress shopping tomorrow if you want to come with me. I'm going to ask Elle to come too. If she does, we will have Max."

"Let me know. I don't think my prison guard will let me go if Max isn't there."

"I'll text you later."

We disconnect the call right as I pull into the driveway. I can't wait to see Ivy. I walk into the house, and Ivy makes a mad dash for me, throwing her hands around my waist, she nearly knocks me to the ground.

"I missed you so much," she yells.

"I missed you too, sweet girl."

"Can we go get a drink? I need to talk to Elle, but you can come too."

She holds my hand on the way to the kitchen where I find Elle cleaning up the kitchen.

"Six weeks Elle. I'm getting married in six weeks."

They both jump up and down ridiculously.

I watch Elle with a blank expression.

"Anyway. Will you be my maid of honor?"

"Oh my GOD!" She yells, "YES!" She covers her mouth as tears run down her face. "I'm so happy that you're marrying my brother."

I smile a toothy grin, "Me too."

"So tomorrow, I was thinking, you, Isabella, and I, go find our dresses or at least try. Once we find mine, we can take Ivy for hers."

Liam walks in wrapping his arms around me and kisses my neck.

"All three of my favorite girls in the same room? I'm a lucky man."

Ivy giggles. She grabs onto his legs, and he lets go of me, squats down, and hugs her tight, making me melt.

"I'm sorry. I'm behind on dinner but I'll start it now."

He wags his finger at me, "You will do no such thing. We are going out for dinner. Your only job is to text Isabella and see if her and Xander would like to join us."

I give him my famous what the fuck look, "I can cook."

"Watch the tone of your eyes. And I'm taking you out. I want to celebrate."

"The tone of my eyes? What are you celebrating?"

He puts his hands on his hips, feigning irritation, "I'm getting married in six weeks to the most beautiful woman in the world. I'm quite happy about it." He smiles, less talking and more texting. I'm getting a drink."

I laugh and text Isabella.

"They will come. But where?"

"La Fontaine's."

I nod, "Okay."

Twenty-Four

LIAM

WE GET TO THE RESTAURANT, and I'm delighted when Ivy whines about sitting with Isabella because I want to be able to touch my girl's hand at the very least. I whisper to her, "You look beautiful, baby girl."

She smiles at me, "Thank you."

Mercy always looks beautiful, but tonight she is wearing this beautiful champagne-colored dress that shows her curves beautifully. It's low cut but not in a sleazy way. Her hair is up in a loose knot exposing her beautiful neck. If we were alone, I'd have my mouth all over it, sucking that sweet spot between her neck and collarbone. This gorgeous woman has me by the balls. There's not a single thing I wouldn't do for her. Her happiness has become my fucking reason for existing.

She blushes when she notices me staring at her, "What?" She asks.

I wink at her, "I like looking at beautiful things."

"You're being quite swoony tonight, Dr. Lexington."

I smirk at her, "Is that a word?"

"Yes, it is. Adjective. Tending to swoon."

I chuckle, "You're something."

She raises an eyebrow, "Didn't they teach you fancy words in medical school, Dr. Lexington?"

I smirk at her, "I guess I missed the day they covered swoony."

She giggles, tossing her head back, and fucking Christ, it makes my heart race.

The waitress brings a round of champagne for everyone and a Shirley Temple for Ivy.

Xander stands up, "I'd like to make a speech and a toast."

I groan, "Here we go."

Xander laughs loud, "Doc Delicious. I never thought you would meet someone like Mercy. You are one lucky son of a-"

"Xander. Little ears," Mercy interrupts.

He rolls his eyes, "You are a lucky man. Do not mess it up!"

Isabella laughs at his change of words.

"To Liam and Mercy. May your wedding be everything the bride wishes for it to be."

Everybody yells, "To Liam and Mercy!"

Mercy blushes and takes a drink of my champagne.

Elle asks, "So where is the wedding?"

Liam shrugs, "We haven't decided."

"Actually, I was hoping you'd be okay with the Butterfly Conservatory in the Rose Garden."

Ivy jumps up and down in her seat, "It's stunning there."

Isabella laughs, "Stunning?"

Ivy glances over at her, "Have you been there?"

She shakes her head, "No, I have not."

Ivy gives her a serious look, "Then you don't know. It's stunning."

Isabella looks at Mercy, biting her lip, trying not to laugh. Mercy raises an eyebrow, "It is. Plus, it holds special memories for us."

I take her hand, "That's where you want to get married?"

She nods, "Only if you'll be happy getting married there."

I chuckle, "I'd marry you anywhere. If that's where you want to get married, then that's where we'll get married."

Her lips hover over my ear, and she whispers, "You better be careful not to spoil me too much. I might become a brat."

I give her a pointed look, "Oh try it, baby girl. See how that works out for you."

She swallows hard and bites her lip.

Finally, our food comes, and it looks delicious. There's a little bit of everything, steak, chicken, shrimp, scallops, pork loin, the options are endless. An endless spread of vegetables, potatoes, and rice. And fresh bread. What is it about warm fresh bread that soothes the soul?

Mercy glances at me with a questioning expression.

"After you sent me the text telling me six weeks, I called and made reservations and ordered."

She smiles, "Thank you."

Mercy glances at Max saying, "Max, would you please eat with us? I'm quite sure you can watch Elle while eating. You make me nervous sitting there all-"

I laugh, "Stony?"

She rolls her eyes, "Yeah. Stony."

Max looks at Elle, "Yes, Max, please eat with us."

Mercy glares at Elle, "Why didn't you say something?"

She shrugs, "I guess I'm used to it."

Elle says, "Tomorrow, I will pick you up after Isabella. Is that okay?"

"Yes," Mercy nods, "I have to take Ivy to school first."

I look at Mercy with a questioning look.

"Dress shopping, baby."

Elle blurts out, "You aren't invited Li Li!"

Everyone laughs at my fallen expression.

"We have to go. Ivy has school tomorrow."

"I want to go look at pretty dresses," she pouts.

"Well, you have school. Also, we can't look for yours until I find mine because I want them to match."

She beams as she claps excitedly.

I pay the bill, which was expensive, but my baby is worth it, and we leave. Hugs and kisses are given on our way out. Mostly to Ivy. Everyone loves her, and it warms my heart. I love that she fits in so well with everyone. She doesn't seem to annoy them like little kids often do. They adore her almost as much as Mercy and I do, almost.

On the drive home, I glanced at her, "Do I need a tux?"

She bites her lip, and I raise an eyebrow. Clearing her throat, she says, "Sorry, I was imagining you in a tux. But you can wear a suit if you prefer."

"What about the honeymoon?"

She beams at me, "I hadn't thought about it. But it would be nice to go somewhere if we can find someone to watch Ivy. It would have to be Elle. I don't want her without us at Isabella and Xander's until this stalker situation is over."

I nod, "Yeah, that makes sense. Where do you want to go?"

Mercy shrugs, "Anywhere with you will be wonderful. I'll let you decide."

I chuckle, "Motel 6 in Stroudsburg it is then!"

She lightly taps my leg, "Okay, maybe not anywhere."

"How long?" I ask.

"I don't know. I'll talk to Elle tomorrow and let you know."

I squeeze her thigh as I pull into the garage.

We walk inside, and Ivy yawns.

Mercy giggles, "Go get pajamas on and brush your teeth. I'll be in shortly to read you a book."

"Okay," she says as she walks sleepily to her bedroom.

Mercy turns to me, "Is the handsome doctor coming to read the book with us?"

"Handsome huh?"

"Oh very, the handsomest."

"I'm going to need a dictionary around you, because I am not sure handsomest is a word."

I pull her into my arms and kiss her neck.

"It is indeed a word, doctor."

"Not one I've ever heard," I say as I bite her neck.

She giggles, "Story time first."

"Oh good, I love reading books about princesses."

She pulls out of my arms and grabs my hand, "This isn't the smutty kind, Liam."

I laugh as she pulls me to Ivy's room.

We all cuddle on Ivy's small bed and read "The Princess and the

Unicorn" which Ivy picked out. She listens attentively to every single word, even though I know she's exhausted.

"Which was your favorite?" She asks me, I think, testing me to see if I was paying attention.

"I liked them both, but I think Juniper was my favorite."

Excitedly she says, "Me too! I like Olivia too, but Juniper is six. I am six."

I chuckle, "Maybe that's why she was my favorite."

"Am I your favorite?" She asks me.

I brush her hair from her face, "You will always be my favorite princess."

She wraps her arms around my neck and squeezes me tight.

My heart is about ready to explode at this moment.

I kiss her on the forehead, "Goodnight, princess. Sweet dreams."

Mercy kisses her and squeezes her tight, and we leave her for what will hopefully be a restful sleep.

Twenty-Five

LIAM

I **GET** undressed while I watch her remove her clothes. Fuck, she's so beautiful. I can't take my eyes off her.

My eyes travel up and down her body, drinking her in. Every fucking curve on her body is perfect. She licks her lips as she does the same to me, but she doesn't speak a word. She pulls the blankets down on the bed and climbs in. I stand by the bed, watching her like an animal might watch its prey.

When she spreads her legs and starts rubbing her clit, I think I might explode on the spot. Walking to the closet, I grab a bag of supplies I bought today, without speaking a word.

She eyes the bag but doesn't stop.

I move to the foot of the bed to get a better view.

When she moans, I nearly lose control.

I grab my cock and stroke it slowly as I watch her insert two fingers into her pussy.

"Daddy," she whimpers.

"Yes, baby girl. Fuck yourself."

This is the most beautiful sight in the world. My girl, so lost in her pleasure. She takes her other hand and rubs her little nub. Her breathing gets ragged, her nipples hard as stone, while her moaning increases. I know she's close.

Her back arches off the bed as her eyes close.

"Such a good girl. Feel it, baby."

As she comes down, I climb on the bed over her.

"Fucking, good girl," I growl.

I yank her fingers out of her as I bury my face between her legs and feast on her, moaning the whole time. She tastes divine, like the sweetest honey. I can't get enough of it. I slide my tongue inside her, and she writhes beneath me. I know exactly where my girl's 'G' spot is. I don't have to guess, so I go right to it, attacking it with everything I have until she's trembling and crying out.

After she comes down from another orgasm, I move her to her side.

"Put your knees to your chest."

I slide into her wet heat, and she moans for me.

Fuck, I love every sound this woman makes.

"You like that, baby girl?"

"YES!" She cries out.

I place my hands on either side of her, thrusting into her hard, rough, just the way she likes it.

She's still tight as hell, and I love it. Lifting her hand up, she pinches her nipple, and I nearly come right then.

"Fuck. You feel so good."

"Daddy, fuck me harder. PLEASE!"

I pick myself up a bit, place one hand under her hip on the bed and my other on her hip up in the air and fuck her harder.

I slam into her repeatedly, and she goes fucking wild.

She digs her fingers into the sheets as she convulses beneath me, speaking incoherent sentences.

"Get on your hands and knees," I command as I pull out.

I grab her hips and slam into her.

"Who owns this pussy?"

"You do," she whimpers.

"Good girl."

I grab the pink butt plug from the bag, squirt lube on, and insert it into her back hole, causing her to cry out.

I work her ass with the toy while I fuck her pussy, and she pushes back, enjoying every second.

"Come for Daddy."

I watch my cock slide in and out of her, and fuck, it makes me crazy. The sound of our bodies slapping together fills the room.

I pull the toy out of her ass, "Daddy!" She cries as her pussy clenches down on my cock so tight it pulls my orgasm from me without warning. I come so hard it almost hurts.

"Fuck, baby girl. Fuck."

I get up and wash the toy. When I come back, I just stare at her. Her cheeks are flushed, her hair has fallen down, and she looks so fucking beautiful.

Mercy

Getting Ivy ready for school is far more of a fight than I realized it would be. After asking her to get dressed nine times, she finally complies. At least I don't have to worry about breakfast because they supply that at school.

"Get your shoes on, please. I don't want you to be late on your first day."

Liam is running out the door, "I love you."

No kiss. He is in a hurry, I guess.

"Have a great day at school!" He yells to Ivy.

I take Ivy to school, and she's so nervous.

"What if nobody likes me?"

"I bet you will make friends today. You're a very sweet girl, Ivy. They are going to like you, a lot. I'm sure of it. Just be yourself."

I see her rolling her eyes in the mirror, "I can't be anyone else."

This little girl. She cracks me up; of course, she has no clue how cute she is.

I drop her off, and her teacher is waiting outside at the pickup line. I hug her and wish her a great day. I hope she settles in and starts to like it because today she did not want to go.

When I get home, Elle and Isabella are there already with Max.

I get out and get into the vehicle that Elle is driving, one of Xander's, a black Range Rover.

We spend hours going from bridal shop to bridal shop. We found their dresses almost instantly, mine, not so much. As we approach the last shop for the day, Elle proclaims, "This is it. I feel it in my bones."

I laugh, "Well, if you feel it in your bones..."

She giggles, loops her arm in mine, and we walk into Stella's Formals. It's a small, independently owned store with circular white couches and flowers everywhere.

As soon as I walk in, I find my dress and Ivy's.

"Oh my God."

Isabella and Elle follow my line of sight to two mannequins, an adult female, and a child. The dresses have identical material, except the little girl doesn't have a train, and instead of a plunging neckline, it covers up to the top of the chest. It's stunning.

"Can I help you?"

"I have an appointment, but I want to try that dress on."

She smiles, "Good choice. Plunging neckline, chapel length train, embellished with lace throughout."

"Size eight in normal clothes?"

I nod, "Impressive."

"You'll need to try a ten or twelve in bridal wear. Let me grab them for you."

She takes me to a changing room, "Here put this on."

It's a white corset. I put it on and yell for help, so Elle comes and fastens it up.

"You must be Mercy," the shop owner says, "I'm Stella."

I smile as she helps me into the dress, which is not easy. I swear it weighs twenty pounds.

It fits like a glove. I smile, all teary-eyed when my phone goes off.

"Elle, can you get my phone? I want to check and make sure that wasn't the school."

She hands me my phone, and I see a text from Liam.

Daddy: Baby girl, I'm sorry but I don't know when or if I'll be home tonight. I need to stay here. I have a little boy that's not doing so well. I need to stay close.

Me: Oh. I'm sorry about your patient. I hope he'll be okay. I miss you.

Isabella sees my face and asks, "Is everything okay?"

"Yeah, I guess. Liam isn't coming home tonight. There's a patient that isn't doing well, so he's staying at the hospital."

"You look upset," Elle says.

"He's never done that before. And he was kind of weird when he left this morning."

I shake my head, "I'm sure it's fine."

"Why don't you go to the hospital and see him after Ivy is in bed? I'll come over and stay with her," Elle said.

"Thank you. I appreciate that. I think I will."

"Is that the dress?" Stella asks.

I nod, "Yes, it definitely is."

She brings me a couple of veils to try, and I fall in love with one that matches so well, finger-tip length with lace around the edges. They look like they were made for each other, but I am told its two different designers.

I get dressed and order it as well as the one for Ivy.

"I'll need to bring her in to try it on though. She won't have it any other way."

"Anytime, dear."

We spent the entire day shopping and laughing. I bought my lingerie for my wedding day and honeymoon. I called and booked the Butterfly Conservatory. We had a lovely lunch where Elle declared we must have a girls' night soon. It was a very productive day, and I am on cloud nine. I'm going to marry the man of my dreams.

They drop me off at home, so I can drive to pick up Ivy. When I get there, she comes running to me, talking a mile a minute about her day. I smile in the mirror at her as I drive away.

"I had so much fun."

"I'm so glad."

"I painted you a picture in art. My art teacher said that I am advanced."

I giggle, "You are. Most kids your age can't do what you can."

She claps excitedly.

When we get home, she goes to her bedroom to play, while I start dinner.

I still haven't gotten a response from Liam, which is strange. So, I decided to text him while the meatloaf bakes.

Me: I found my wedding gown! I miss you terribly.

No response. I'll see him soon and find out what's going on, so I push it out of my mind as I finish dinner.

Elle shows up just before dinner and eats with us. I bathe Ivy and read her a book before heading out. But my mind is on Liam.

He doesn't lose patients often, but I'm concerned that maybe he did.

When I put Ivy to bed, Elle looks at me, "You know he wouldn't cheat on you, right?"

"I know that. I'm concerned that something happened."

She nods, "Okay. I was afraid you thought he wasn't at the hospital and was with another woman."

"No. Not at all. But Liam normally responds to me, and he hasn't."

"Go," she says.

I nod, "I won't be long. I just want to make sure he's okay."

Twenty-Six

LIAM

IT'S BEEN A LONG DAY, and I'm exhausted. I want nothing more than to go home and be with Mercy. But I can't. I must first see how this little boy does on the new medication. If he responds well, then I can leave. I let the nurses know I'm going to the on-call room for a little while and to call me if anything changes.

I walk in, take my shoes and shirt off, and climb into bed to get a little sleep.

I'm dead to the world when something hits me in the head.

Sitting up instantly, I see Mercy in the doorway with tears running down her face. Then I look to my right. What the fuck? Nurse Stephanie is naked beside me.

Mercy shakes her head as she turns to walk away.

Fuck. Fuck. Fuck.

I grab my shirt and shoes and put them on to go after Mercy. I look at Stephanie and tell her, "I'll be talking to your Unit Manager, you're done here."

When I walk into the hall, Mercy is gone. I walk out to the parking lot, and she's not there. She had already left. I can't leave my patient. This is a fucking nightmare, my worst nightmare.

I fetch my phone out of my pocket, and I missed a text from her which I know just makes it look worse.

I called her, but it went to voicemail which I pretty much expected.

I send her a text.

Me: I did nothing with her. I don't know why she was in my bed. I was sleeping and not naked. Please talk to me. I can't leave right now.

I walk back into the hospital and check on my patient again. My hands are tied. As much as I want to go home to fix this, I can't. I'm stuck here until I don't even know when.

Approximately forty minutes later, I get a text, but it's not the one I've been hoping for.

Elle: You fucking idiot. How could you?

Me: I didn't. I don't know why she was in my bed.

Elle: You'll need to come up with something much better than that. Liam, she loves you so much. Why?

Me: I'm telling the truth, Elle. Is she at the house?

Elle: Yeah, she is because Ivy is here otherwise, she'd already be gone. Can you blame her?

I call Mercy again, but it goes straight to voicemail.

Me: I need to talk to her.

Elle: She's too busy sobbing to take your call. She shut her phone off.

Me: I would never cheat on her.

My heart breaks at the thought of her crying because she thinks I cheated on her. She's everything to me. Why the hell would I want another woman? FUCK!

I search for Stephanie's Unit Manager and catch him just as he's getting ready to leave.

I explain what happened to Michael and tell him I want her gone. It's sexual harassment. He's shocked but says he'll need to do an investigation. I check on my patient, and he seems to be stabilizing, which I'm grateful for. His heart rate was dropping rapidly. It's still too low, but it's rising. So, I need to wait a little longer to see if it returns to normal. I believe it will, but the waiting is killing me for more than one reason.

I go back to the on-call room and sit in silence.

Mercy could have any man that she wanted. I know I'm probably going to lose her. I am not an idiot; I know exactly what it looked like—the look on her face. Shit, I'll never get it out of my head.

Finally, my patient's heart rate is normal so that I can leave. I will get a call if it gets worse again, I head home. The entire way home, I attempt to figure out what I'm going to say to her to make this right. I did nothing wrong; I know that. That doesn't make me feel better because I know Mercy thinks I had sex with her. I didn't, I wouldn't, but how do I make her believe it? I don't have a fucking clue. I can't lose her. My stomach churns thinking about it. I pull into my driveway, and I still don't have a plan.

I walk in and go straight to the bedroom since she's probably in bed. I see the most gut-wrenching sight I could have imagined and did imagine. An empty bed. My girl isn't here, my chest hurts. She's gone? What about Ivy? Did she take her and leave?

I blow out a deep breath. *Relax, Liam. Maybe she's in another room.* I go to Ivy's room; the door is closed. I open it quietly and breathe a sigh of relief when I see Ivy fast asleep in bed. I move to the first of several guest rooms. I open the door, and Mercy is lying in bed sobbing.

I was wrong before; this is the most gut-wrenching sight. I sit beside her on the bed and touch her shoulder, she flinches.

"Don't fucking touch me."

"Baby girl, I didn't do anything."

"Get out, Liam."

I rest my elbows on my knees, my face in my hands, she repeats herself, "Get out, Liam."

"I can't, Mercy."

"What do you mean you can't?"

I feel the bed shift when she sits up.

"I can't be without you. I can't fucking sleep without you."

Through her sobs, she says, "You should have considered that before you destroyed me."

"I went into the room, took my shoes off and my shirt and climbed into bed. It had been a hard day, I was exhausted. I woke up when something hit me on my head. You were standing there, and she was beside me. I never fucking touched her, Mercy."

"Just go."

"Just go?"

I stand furious, "Did I ever mean a fucking thing to you?"

She glares at me, "You're asking me that?"

"God damn it, Mercy. You're pissing me off. I have never been anything but completely honest with you. I have always taken care of you and put your needs before my own. Tell yourself whatever the fuck you want to get out of this. But I've treated you like a fucking queen."

I can't stand another minute in a room with her, so I go to my bedroom. Not ours, apparently. Mine.

I get out of my scrubs, throw them in the washer, and climb into bed, alone. I guess I may as well get used to it. My mind is in overdrive. I've lost Mercy. I'm going to lose Ivy. My parents are dead. My son is in fucking prison. I've lost everything. A tear rolls down my cheek. What the fuck? I don't cry, ever. I'm lying in my giant bed when my phone chimes.

Elle: Are you okay?

Me: Nope.

Elle: I'm sorry I was so rough on you. I know you. If you say you didn't do anything with her, I believe you.

Me: She doesn't. It's over.

Elle: Giver her time.

Me: No. I told her exactly what happened, and she told me to get out.

Elle: She told you to get out of your own house?

Me: The guest bedroom. She's sleeping there.

Elle: Oh shit.

Me: It's done. It was beautiful while it lasted—time to move on.

Elle: Liam, you have to work it out.

Me: There's nothing to work out. It's as if she was looking for a reason and got the perfect one. I'm done. Going to bed. Love you, Cupcake.

I'm a liar. I'm not going to bed. I can't fucking sleep without her wrapped around me, and it pisses me off. After hours of tossing and turning, I fall asleep. I wake up the happiest man in the world with

Mercy on top of me. Her scent surrounds me, her lips brush mine, her hair tickles my shoulder, and then I open my eyes. It was a fucking dream. She's not here. FUCK!

I hear them in the kitchen, which means I have to play nice for Ivy's sake. I go into the kitchen to get coffee to take it back to my bedroom. I get my coffee, and Ivy asks me to sit at the table with her, so she can show me the painting she did at school.

"I'll be right there, Princess."

I take a sip of my coffee when Mercy says to me, "I hope you slept well, Liam."

I glare at her, "I did not."

She glares right back, "Pity."

I smile for Ivy's benefit, "You're lucky Ivy is here."

"Why, you'd get your belt?" She smirks.

I whisper in her ear, "In your fucking dreams. I won't ever touch you again with anything."

Half a second later, when she ran to the bedroom crying, I regret what I said. Fuck. Why did I have to say that? To Mercy, of all people. That's the problem with words. Once they are said, no matter how much you regret them, they can never be taken back.

I sit with Ivy, and her painting, as usual, it's stunning.

There's a house with a bright sun, two adults and a small child. I already know it's a family portrait. A family that I'll never be able to give Ivy. Chances are, she will be taken from us when they find out what's happening. The one thing she needs more than anything right now is stability. I wanted us to be the ones to give that to her.

Mercy comes out of the bedroom and says to Ivy, "Ready?"

Ivy excitedly jumps up, comes over to me, and kisses me on the cheek.

When Mercy goes towards the door, Ivy says, "You have to kiss him too."

She walks over to me as I smirk and goes to kiss me on the cheek. I grab the back of her neck and kiss her on the lips. She doesn't kiss me back. The pain in my chest is excruciating.

Twenty-Seven

LIAM

MY LIFE HAS TURNED into a fucking shit show. I did get a text from Gloria saying Stephanie had been fired. So, at least that went my way, but what I wanted most of all was for Mercy to believe me. Would I have believed her if the roles had been reversed? Probably not. She saw me in bed with a naked woman.

I get ready for work and leave as my phone starts ringing through my Bluetooth.

"Hey Javier, what's up?"

"When you get in, can you come see me before you start rounds?"

"Yeah, sure. I'm on my way now."

"Okay, boss."

I chuckle as I disconnect the call. I'm not his boss, although I did get him his job. Javier is great at what he does. He's the IT Director now, after starting as a Help Desk Technician.

After my short drive to the hospital, I walk into his office and sit beside him. He's doing something, so I wait.

"I have a video for you to watch and then you need to explain."

It starts when I see the number six outside of a door, on-call room six. I wait.

Stephanie approaches the door and looks around her, left to right,

right to left several times. She looks like she's up to no good. Then she goes into the room and closes the door behind her. He fast forwards, "Fifteen minutes," he says.

Mercy comes in.

"I've seen enough. Don't make me watch this."

He pauses the screen.

"What the hell happened? Stephanie was fired and I heard nurses talking today saying you're available again."

"I am not fucking available. She climbed into my bed, I was sleeping, Mercy came in and of course believed the worst. The end."

"Why was Stephanie fired?"

"Sexual Harassment."

"Now what?" He asks, his hands folded on his lap.

"Nothing."

He raises an eyebrow, "This girl means everything to you. I can get the paperwork for you to show that Stephanie was fired."

"There's no point. Mercy saw me in bed with a naked woman. We can't ever move on from that."

I stand and go to leave, very done with this conversation. "Thanks for caring, man. I need to get to rounds."

He sighs, "Alright, boss."

Mercy

I need to check in with Maria at the hospital to see if I can return to work part-time. Everything with Liam is a mess, and all this free time is driving me insane. I didn't want Ivy to go to school today because I couldn't bear to be alone with my never-ending thoughts.

I'm sitting on the couch flipping through the options on Netflix when my phone starts ringing.

"Hello," I answer.

"Mercy Madison, please."

"Speaking."

I lay back on the couch in what used to be our spot as I listened to the man on the phone.

"This is Javier from IT at PCH."

"Okay?" I respond in a questioning manner.

"Can you come see me today? The earlier the better?"

I frown at the phone, "You do realize I don't work there anymore, right?"

"Can you come in?" He asks.

I shake my head, "Sure."

"Do you know where IT is?"

"I do."

I saw it and met him when I got the hospital tour.

I get up and get ready, wondering what on earth he wants with me. I shower, get changed, and drive to the hospital.

When I get to the hospital, I park and walk to the IT department, hoping I don't run into Liam. This morning was painful and stressful. At this moment, I'm hoping he'll be working late, which I know is wrong because Ivy will want to see him.

I knock on the open door and walk in.

"Can you close the door, please?"

I nod and shut it.

"Sit, please."

He hands me a folder, "I'd appreciate this conversation to be kept confidential because I could lose my job over this. But Liam has helped me, and now it's my turn to help him.

"Oh, this is about Liam," I hand him the folder and go to stand.

"Don't you even want to know the truth?"

I stare at him, unsure of how to even respond.

"The truth is, there in that folder. Don't you owe it to yourself to at least know?"

I take the folder back and sit back down.

I read:

Stephanie Jacobs. Dr. Shane Jacobs' sister. What the fuck?

Stephanie Jacobs Statement:

I went into the on-call room where Dr. Lexington was sleeping. My brother asked me to do it because he's fascinated with Dr. Lexington's fiancé. He said the nurses would talk, and Liam would lose everything. I got undressed, and he was sleeping deeply. I climbed into bed with him. He moaned Mercy a few times but never woke up until the woman entered the room and threw his shoe at his head. Nothing happened between us. He did not even know I was there until his fiancé walked into the room, waking him up.

Then I lost my job for sexual harassment. I'm writing this statement being honest and truthful to hopefully not lose my license.

Dr. Shane Jacobs:

Employment ended due to admitting involvement in sexual harassment. Signed by Chief of Medicine Daniel Darby.

There's so much more, but I've seen enough.

"Is Liam aware of all of this?"

He nods.

"Why didn't he tell me?"

A frown crosses his features, "He thinks after what you saw that there's no coming back from it. I don't think Liam believes you love him at this point if I'm honest. I'm crossing a line, but I thought you deserved to know the truth."

I smile weakly, "Thank you. I appreciate this."

I hand him the folder and leave.

After walking to the cancer wing, I find Gloria. "Where's Dr. Lexington?"

"He's in with a patient," she responds.

I smile, "I'll wait if that's okay."

"Of course," she says, "It's good to see you."

She makes small talk as I scroll through my phone. But really, I only have one thing on my mind.

Liam comes to the nurse's desk, and my heart starts rapidly firing.

"Mercy, why are you here?"

I look down, "I need to talk to you."

"Is Ivy, okay?" He sounds panicked.

"She's fine. Can we talk for a minute?"

"I'm sure it can wait until later tonight," he says dryly.

"It really can't."

He runs his hand through his hair, "Fine. Follow me to the consultation room."

I do and say, "The on-call rooms are closer."

"Yeah, I don't like being in them anymore."

He opens the door and waves me in.

After closing the door, he says, "What do you need?"

"You," I said.

"Mercy. What are you doing?" He says as I wrap my arms around him.

"Javier called me."

"He what?"

"He asked me to come in, and he showed me the file on Stephanie and Shane."

"Shane?" He asks.

"He asked her to do it."

I stand on my toes and pull his head down and lick his lips, he groans.

"I'm so mad at you," he says.

"Kiss me, anyway."

I press my lips to his, and at first, he doesn't respond, he's fighting it. I know damn well he wants to kiss me back.

When I bite his bottom lip, he loses the fight.

He pulls my hair aggressively and plunges his tongue into my mouth as he growls. Fuck, I love that growl.

He moves from my lips to my jaw, to my neck, devouring me like a starving man. He bites my neck as his hands move down my back to my ass.

"Why couldn't you believe me?" His voice sounds pained. "I would never betray you."

"Because finding you with a naked woman made anything you said unbelievable."

He steps back from me and shakes his head.

"Liam, I love you."

He blows out a big breath, "I'll always love you, Mercy. Until the day I stop breathing."

He walks out of the room, closing the door behind him.

Twenty-Eight

LIAM

SHE BELIEVES ME. She knows I didn't cheat on her. It's everything I wanted since she walked into that fucking room. Why am I so angry with her for not believing me without proof? I know I would've been heartbroken if I found her like that. And the excuse 'it's not what it looks like' would not have flown. The truth is, I'm so fucking angry with her, whether it's rational or not. I wanted to not kiss her back so badly, just leave her in that room without ever touching her. My body can't say no to her, whether I'm pissed or not. I was two seconds away from angry fucking her, which would have been too rough and painful even for Mercy. If I had done to her what I wanted to do, it probably would've been over for sure. I wanted so badly to remove my belt and spank the hell out of her. But that's a hard limit for her, so I can't. Instead, I did the responsible thing and walked away.

I text Xander.

Me: I could really use a drink. Are you in surgery tonight?

Xander: No, I'm done for the day in about an hour.

Me: *On-Call Room* at five?

Xander: Sounds good.

After checking on my other patients, I checked in with Michael one last time. His heart rate scared me. I honestly thought we were going to lose him. I haven't lost many patients, and one is far too many.

"Hey buddy, how are you feeling?"

"Better," he smiles shyly.

I look at his parents, who have sat at his bedside the entire time. They are never both gone at the same time.

"I hope you're taking care of yourselves as well."

His mom smiles, "I'm fine now. I think I died a thousand deaths yesterday though. Thank you for staying and making sure our boy was okay."

I grab his chart to look through the most recent results of his EKG.

"My pleasure," I respond to her while assessing the data.

"Much better," I said.

"Is he going to be, okay?" His mom asks.

I grin, "I think so. But I do want a pediatric cardiologist to come take a look. I was able to prescribe medication to regulate his heart rate but I'm not a heart specialist. So, let's have an expert in and see what she thinks."

She nods, "Of course, thank you doctor."

"You're welcome."

"Now, Michael. I want you to stay in bed until the heart doctor sees you, okay?"

He groans, expectedly. They never want to hear that. "Nurse Gloria will bring you a tablet to keep you occupied. But we can't be too careful. If the specialist says you can go to the playroom, then I'm fine with it. But until then let's play it safe."

He rolls his eyes but says, "Fine."

I tap his leg, "Alright kiddo. I'll see you tomorrow."

"Bye," he says.

He's annoyed with me, but I will not take the risk of him over-exerting his heart and something terrible happening. I say goodbye to his parents, who will undoubtedly be here when I see him next.

I say goodbye to Nurse Gloria after asking her to get Michael a tablet. Then I head out to meet with Xander, who I'm hoping will help me make sense of my head.

Traffic is light, so I make it to the bar in less time than expected.

I walk in and head straight to Xander's favorite booth, which is strange because who has a favorite booth?

I slide in on the other side of him.

"Hey asshole," he says.

"Sometimes you hurt my feelings."

He chuckles, "Oh Jesus. What has she done to you Doc Delicious?"

"One of these days I'm going to hit you. And the Doc Delicious thing. Yeah, even less funny with Stephanie."

I tell him the entire story about Stephanie and her brother Shane. How everything went with Mercy, and what happened in the consultation room earlier today. As always, he mostly sits and listens attentively.

"You're angry that she didn't just take you at your word, immediately?"

I take a deep breath, "She didn't take my word for it. It wasn't until she saw it in Stephanie's own words that she believed me. I'm supposed to forget the rest and I can't."

He shakes his head, "You're a fucking idiot."

"Why thank you," I reply dryly.

"She found you in bed with a naked woman."

"I didn't fucking touch her."

He rubs the scruff on his chin, "Liam, I fucking know that man. Settle down. But think from her perspective. You walk in and find her shirtless with a naked man next to her. She swears it's not what it looks like. Are you telling me you would just believe her?"

"No," I hang my head down. This whole situation has me feeling like absolute shit.

"Of course, you wouldn't. She reacted the way any other woman would. If she hadn't, then she wouldn't be the woman I know. She may be submissive in the bedroom, but she'll never be walked all over."

"I've never tried to walk all over her."

He sighs, "I'm going to cut to the chase."

I nod, and he asks, "Do you want to be with Mercy?"

"Obviously."

"Then cut the fucking shit, asshole before you lose her."

"I have no right to be mad, then?"

"At Mercy? Nope. At Stephanie hell-fucking-yes you do."

"Alright."

"You are misplacing your anger. Get your head right before she's gone. You won't find another like her."

"I wouldn't even bother trying."

"Then what are you doing here? It's nine o'clock. Ivy is in bed and you're here with me, while the girl of your dreams is in your house alone."

I stand to get ready to leave, "Thanks. You're a good friend."

He chuckles, "Better than you deserve."

I shake my head and leave.

Driving home, my heart pounds at the thought of seeing Mercy. Can we get through this? We have to because I can't function in a world without her. Somehow, I need to make this right.

I drive down the street and my words to her, *I'll never touch you again*, replay in my mind. Why did I say that? I know why, I was angry. I had lost her, I was pissed, so I lashed out.

When I pull into the driveway, I'm a nervous wreck. What if walking away from her earlier cemented my fate? I walk into the house, and it's dark and quiet. I go into my bedroom hoping to find her in my bed, but she's not. So, I go to the guest room and find her asleep. No, this will not do.

I pull the blankets off her, scoop her into my arms, carry her to my bed, and gently lay her down.

After I get down to my boxers, I crawl into bed and pull her into my arms. Her eyelids flutter open, and her beautiful eyes stare into mine.

"What are you doing?" She asks.

"Going to bed," I respond dryly.

"Why did you bring me in here?"

I brush the hair out of her face and kiss her on the forehead, "Baby girl, you are not a guest. You shouldn't be in the guest room. You belong with me in our bed."

"Liam, I-"

I silence her by pressing my lips to hers. When I swipe her lips with my tongue, she moans, parting her lips, giving me full access to her mouth. I slide my tongue into her mouth, deepening our kiss. She wraps her hands around my neck, pulling me closer. Then she moans into my mouth, and I nearly go insane. One fucking night without this woman feels like a damn lifetime. She's wearing a t-shirt and panties, nothing else. I glide my hand up her thigh, pulling back from our kiss.

"I want to be gentle with you. But I also want to remind you who owns this delicious body. You're mine, baby girl. No matter what, you'll always be mine."

She sits up and takes her shirt off. "Fuck me like you own me then."

Twenty-Nine

LIAM

HIS EYES DARKEN WITH DESIRE. He pushes me down on the bed, wrapping his hand around my throat, "Fuck you like I own you? Challenge accepted, baby girl."

The way he stares at me makes my heart race. My arousal heightens when he cups one breast and licks the nipple of the other.

"So fucking beautiful," he breathes.

He bites down on my bud, and I moan loudly.

"How is it that one night without you is the purest form of torture?"

He drags his fingertips and mouth down my body, kissing my abdomen, his eyes lock on mine.

"Tell me you missed me," he commands.

"I missed you," I say truthfully,

Forcefully, he moves my thighs apart, puts his face over my lace panties, and inhales.

"Your scent drives me fucking wild."

He sits up and pulls my panties down my legs and over my feet.

"I need to taste you. Come on my tongue, baby girl."

"I need you inside me," I whimper.

He growls, "I'll tell you what you fucking need."

He runs his tongue up my slit and back down several times.

"Why would you even think I'd cheat on you? This is the most beautiful, pink pussy I've ever seen. I could never want another."

He plunges his tongue inside of me and thrusts his tongue in and out repeatedly. I moan as I grab onto his hair, bucking my hips.

"Daddy, yes. Oh God."

He pulls his tongue out and says, "Fucking delicious."

When he licks my clit it's an instant orgasm. "FUCK!" I scream as my back arches off the bed. I lose myself in the powerful orgasm hitting me in waves.

"Daddy," I whimper.

He doesn't stop. He moans as he soaks up every ounce of my arousal like a madman.

When he gets up, his face glistens with my wetness.

Without a word, he gets up, places one leg on either side of my head, and slams his cock into my shocked, open mouth.

"Be a good girl, suck my dick, baby."

His dirty talk is next level and never-ending. "You look so good with my cock in your mouth."

He wraps his hands around the headboard and fucks my mouth like a crazy man, staring at my face.

"Yeah, baby girl, you're so good."

When I moan, he moves faster. Tears fill my eyes as he tips his head back, groaning, "FUCK!"

Holy shit. He's always sexy when he comes, but this is the definition of hot.

He pulls out and moves beside me breathing heavily. He brushes my hair from my face.

"You're so stunning."

I smile at him softly when he commands, "Get on your hands and knees."

He goes and gets the lube, and I know what's coming next. We haven't had to use lube since my hysterectomy, so I'm about to get my ass fucked. There was a time when I would have been terrified, but I was excited because I know I will have one hell of an orgasm.

"Spread your legs, baby girl."

I do as he comes up behind me and runs his tongue from the middle of my back down to my ass.

He smacks my ass as he speaks in a husky voice, "Such a sexy ass. Do I own this too, baby girl?"

"Yes," I breathe.

He groans as he licks my back hole.

This man, my man, is so fucking dirty, and I love it.

He slides two fingers in my pussy and his tongue in my ass at the same time, and I cry out in pleasure.

After thrusting a few times, he pulls his tongue and fingers out.

"I have to fuck you, NOW!" He growls.

He gets on his knees and fills me completely with one thrust as he slams into me like a truck.

"You love it when I fuck your cunt, don't you dirty slut?"

"Yes!" I cry out as he pulls my hair forcefully.

He fucks me hard, pushing me forward with every thrust. The sound of our skin slapping, and heavy breathing fills the air.

"Are you going to let me fill that gorgeous ass, baby girl?"

"Yes, Daddy," I breathe.

"Good girl, such a fucking good girl."

He pulls out and gets the lube and spreads some on my back hole, and when I turn my head to look back and see him staring at my ass as he strokes his cock with lube, I nearly combust.

I moan, and he flashes me a sexy grin.

"Do you like that, baby?"

"God, yes."

He lines his cock up and slides into me not fast but also not slow.

We moan together as he begins to move faster.

"Fuck, how can you feel this fucking good?"

He grabs my hips with a bruising grip.

"Do you like it like that, baby girl?"

"Fuck me harder, Daddy."

I liked it just fine, but I know damn well those words will make him lose control. I love Liam when he's in control, but it's everything when he comes undone because of what I do to him.

"Fuck. Say it again," he says as he increases his intensity.

"Fuck me harder, Daddy."

He fucks me like a God. No human being should fuck like this.

His grip tightens on my hips, and he slams into me with the force of a wrecking ball.

"Fucking come, dirty slut. Give it all to me."

I cry out a throaty cry. My arms give out, and my face hits the mattress as I experience an actual toe-curling orgasm that controls my entire body. I'm convulsing and making sounds I've never heard when he breathes my name as if it's a prayer.

He pulls out of me, lifts me in his strong arms, and carries me to the bathroom. Setting me on the counter, he looks at me with a concerned expression, "Are you okay, baby girl?"

I smile, "I'm fine, just tired."

"Bath first, then bed."

We normally take a shower together, but he fills the tub instead.

I nod.

After he's happy with the water level and the bubbles, he picks me up off the counter and carries me into the bathtub with him, he lowers himself, holding me tightly.

"You're being awfully sweet, Dr. Lexington."

He spreads his legs so I can sit between them and holds me to his chest.

"If I can be rough with you, I can also be tender with you."

I giggle, "You once told me you didn't know how to be gentle."

He washes my front as he sighs, "You taught me some things I didn't even know about myself."

"I love you."

"Baby girl, I love you too," his voice cracks, "I can't spend another night without you."

"I'm sorry I didn't believe you."

"After what you saw, how could you possibly? It guts me that you even went through that. I will never cheat on you."

I stand and climb onto his lap, straddling him. I wrap my arms around his neck.

"I know, baby."

Lowering my head, I kiss him softly.

He places his arms around my back, holding me firmly against his chest.

"When I thought I lost you..."

I look up at him, "What were you going to say?"

He runs his hand through his hair, "When I thought I lost you, I didn't even know how to go on. It scared the hell out of me."

He continues kissing me on the forehead, "I can't go through this again, Mercy. I've lost you three fucking times now. Each time it gets harder to handle."

"Maybe sleep in a fucking on-call room with a lock instead of the one that doesn't have one," I bite.

He pulls my hair, "Are you getting sassy with me, baby girl?" He smiles, "Wash my dick."

A giggle bubbles out of me. "What?"

"I'm going to fuck you and I don't want you to get an infection. Wash it."

LIAM

SHE DISPENSES soap into her hands while she watches me with an intense gaze. When she strokes up and down my cock with her sudsy hand, I hiss in response. "Fuck, baby girl."

Once she rinses me off, I motion for her to ride me.

She lowers herself onto my dick and leans forward and bounces. Her tits are in my face, and her scent is all around me as I groan.

"Do you like that, Daddy?"

I catch her one nipple and bite down, and she yelps.

"Fuck yes, I like this."

I grab her hips, "But you're not taking all of me. My dirty slut needs every inch of my cock."

I hold her still and slam into her, making her cry out.

"Good girl, take all of it." I slam into her again. "This fucking cunt was made for me."

"Yes, Daddy, only for you," she breathes.

I loosen my grip on her hips.

"Show me how much you love this cock, baby girl."

She clenches her muscle and squeezes me, forcing me to intake a sharp breath.

"Fuck," I hiss.

Then she rises and slams back down.

I don't know how she stayed a virgin for so long because this girl was made to fuck.

I grab both of her tits, "Good girl, fuck me."

She places her hands on my shoulders and fucks me like a jackhammer.

"Daddy...I'm gonna...I can't hold it..."

Tossing her head back, she clenches my dick like a fucking vice, forcing my orgasm out of me. I grab her waist as she trembles on top of me while I shoot my cum deep inside her.

"Fuck."

She falls forward, collapsing on my chest.

"I think you've had enough for tonight, baby girl. Let's get you to bed."

She responds, "Mhmm," with her eyes closed. My girl is spent. I get out of the tub, dry off quickly, and then grab a towel and put it around her before lifting her in my arms.

"You did so good tonight, baby. You're perfect," I say as I lay her in bed.

When I climb into bed beside her and pull her into my arms, she's already asleep, exactly where she belongs. It takes me a long time to fall asleep because I lay staring at her for so long, relieved we could put things back together.

It's early, and I can feel it when I hear something. I open my eyes and glance at the clock on the nightstand. Six o'clock in the morning, not as early as I thought. I climb out of bed and pull my boxers and pajama pants on so I can investigate the noise, I'm sure it's Ivy. After opening the door quietly, I walk through the hallway towards the kitchen and stop dead in my tracks. She painted my fucking wall! No longer concerned about waking Mercy, I yell, "WHAT ARE YOU DOING?"

She turns to look at me, still wearing her nightgown with a paint-brush in her hand, "I am making butterflies for Mercy."

"ON MY WALL?"

Mercy comes running out, "Why are you yelling?"

I point at the wall, becoming furious by the second when Ivy looks at me, "You don't like it?" Unshed tears fill her eyes, and I feel like shit. The butterflies are well done, she's gifted. BUT MY WALL? Couldn't she use fucking paper?

Mercy looks at me, "You. Go get ready for work. I will handle this. I'll fix your wall. Now go."

Then she looks at Ivy, "Bathroom now. Don't touch a thing."

I blow out a breath and get ready for work—what a way to start the damn day. Twenty minutes later, I'm dressed and go out to the kitchen to get coffee. As I'm sipping my coffee, they come into view. Ivy is all clean and dressed. The paint from her cheek and arms is gone. Mercy takes such good care of her.

Ivy runs over to me, wrapping her arms around me, "I'm sorry. I wanted to make a surprise for Mercy. Please don't be mad."

I set my coffee cup down on the counter and hugged her back.

"It's a beautiful picture and it was quite the surprise. No more wall pictures, okay? Let's stick to paper."

"I'll get paint today to paint over it."

I shake my head, "No. Leave it. But no more after this."

"You want me to leave the butterflies?" She asks with a raised pitch.

"Yeah well, it'll give Xander so much pleasure to mess with me about it. I'd hate to disappoint him."

She giggles, and all is restored in my grumpy heart.

Ivy stares up at me, "Cars?"

I chuckle, "Yes, car scrubs today."

She scrunches up her nose, "I like princesses."

"What are your plans today?" I glance at Mercy.

"I'm taking Ivy to school and then running to the hospital to see Maria. After Ivy is done with school, we are going to the dress shop, so she can try on the dress I picked out for her."

I smile broadly, "I'm sure she will enjoy that. Why are you seeing Maria?"

I'm pretty sure they aren't friends. Maria is the Supervisor of the social workers in the cancer ward.

"I want to talk to her to see if it's possible for me to come back part time, during the hours when Ivy is in school."

"The kids need someone like you. If you need me to talk to her-"

She shakes her head as she interrupts me, "No. I want to do this myself."

I sigh, "Very well, baby girl."

"Do you have time for breakfast?" She asks, walking into the kitchen and grabbing bacon and eggs from the refrigerator.

"Thank you, but I don't. Text me when you're done with Maria. If I have time, we can have coffee."

She giggles, "Don't you get sick of seeing me, Dr. Lexington?"

I raise an eyebrow at her, "Surprisingly, I don't."

I squat down near Ivy, counting the eggs, "Give me a hug, Princess. I'll see you later tonight."

She turns to me and hugs me, "I love you," she squeals.

I am a little shocked by her words but respond, "I love you too. Have a good day at school."

Then I stand and move over to Mercy. I pull her into my arms, unafraid of the egg in her hand, and kiss her neck.

"You're lucky I feel nice today, or you'd have broken egg all over you."

I give her a serious expression, "That would be an instant ten. Choose wisely, baby girl."

She gasps, "Ten?"

"Yes, ten," I respond flatly.

Reaching over, she places the egg back in the carton and wraps her arms around my neck.

"Good girl."

I kiss her far quicker than I like because Ivy is standing next to us watching.

"I love you. Have a good day."

"I love you too," she breathes.

Reluctantly, I pull away and head for the door to go to work when really, I just want to fall back into bed with my girl.

I open the door to my Escalade and spot a CD sitting on my seat with a note stuck to it.

"Wedding songs," the note reads.

I smile as I get into my car and put the CD in to listen on my drive.

I never saw marriage in my cards. I didn't have anything against it, and I just knew it wasn't for me. Or I thought it wasn't for me. That was before Mercy, however. I can't imagine not marrying her. Not long now, and she'll be my wife. I'm probably the only man this excited about a wedding. But it's not the wedding I'm looking forward to, it's the mere fact that she'll be mine, permanently.

I listen to my girl's CD as I drive down the highway. I smile to myself as I pull into my parking spot.

I remember the first time we came to the hospital together when she met Ivy for the first time. I never imagined this was where we would end up when I tried so hard not to touch her. If I'm honest with myself, something about her grabbed onto me in the bar and wouldn't let go. When I found her naked in my bathroom, I was done. It didn't matter how hard I fought, eventually, I'd lose the fight, and I did. Right now, I'm grateful for her persistence. I can't imagine my life without her.

I head into the hospital to start my rounds.

My first patient is little Michael with heart issues. I read his chart before heading in to see what the pediatric cardiologist had to say.

I sigh as I walk into his room. It's not great news.

"Michael, buddy. How are you feeling?"

"Sick," he responds.

I sit beside his bed as I smile at his mother.

"Have you been throwing up?"

His mom gets up and hands me a paper.

I look down at it and smile as I realize this is a record of this kid's vomit. She's keeping track of it.

"This is helpful, thank you."

Man, this kid has been vomiting nearly around the clock.

"Do the nurses know?" I ask his mom.

She shakes her head, "No. Not to the extent that he has been."

"Okay, next time let them know. They could call me, and I could prescribe something different which I will now."

I glance at Michael, "I'm going to get you some medicine for your belly. We already had you on something for a sick stomach. This will work better but it might make you sleepy."

Again, I look to his mom, "A nurse will be coming by every three hours today to ask how frequently he's vomiting. They will do that until we get this under control. Of course, the nausea is expected, however, this is more than we expect. I want the weight loss kept to a minimum. Have them call me if you need anything."

She smiles, "Thank you, doctor."

Thirty-One

MERCY

I'M SITTING in Maria's office while she tries to get me to come back full-time.

"I can't. We have Ivy now; she needs me home with her after school."

She sighs, "So, if I tell you the only way you can come back is full-time, you'd say no?"

I nod, "I would. It's not an option for me right now. Ivy has to come first, no one has done that before. It's what she needs."

"What hours can you work then?"

She sits with a scowl on her face, her hands tapping on her desk as if there are a million other things, I'm keeping her from.

"Nine until two."

She sighs, "Fine. Can you start tomorrow?"

Oh boy. This isn't going to go well. I can feel it.

"Rather than asking for time off right away, I thought it best to start after our honeymoon."

She rolls her eyes, "Right. Just let me know the date you can start, and I'll get the paperwork ready."

I smile sweetly, "Thank you so much, Maria. I'm excited."

As I stand to leave, she says, "Ivy's mom knows you and Liam have her."

I snap my head back towards her in surprise, "What?"

She nods, "She called and asked me for your address, which obviously I did not give her."

Shit. Why does she want to know where we live? She's not allowed to see Ivy. We are in the process of her losing her parental rights so we can adopt her.

I sigh, "Thank you for telling me."

She smiles, but it doesn't reach her eyes, "Have a nice day."

I text Liam as I leave her office.

Me: I'm done with Maria. Ivy's mom contacted her to find out our address.

Daddy: What? Tell me she didn't give it to her.

Me: No. She didn't. But what does she want?

Daddy: Meet me in the coffee shop. I'll be there in ten.

I make my way to the coffee shop, grab a cup for both of us, and sit at the table waiting for Liam. I'm freaking out inside. Is she going to try to challenge us? The thought of Ivy going back to her makes me feel sick to my stomach. Surely, they wouldn't give a child back to an abusive parent, right? Wrong. I saw it more than once during my internship with CPS. Frequently, what's easiest for the people involved, rather than what's best for the child, is what's done. This is what you get with an overworked system. And case workers with caseloads far larger than they should ever have.

Liam comes in with a concerned expression on his face. He walks over to me, kisses me on the forehead, and then sits down at our small table.

"Coffee," I hand him his cup.

"Thank you, baby girl. Are you okay?"

I bite my lip and nod.

"I'm concerned, obviously. I wonder what she wants and I'm worried that she might try to get her back."

"I will contact our lawyer. We'll try to get an earlier hearing date."

I smile, "Thank you."

"It'll be okay, baby girl. I promise. You won't lose Ivy."

He brushes my hair out of my face and strokes my cheek staring at me with those eyes that make me weak. Leaning forward, he kisses me softly.

"What did Maria say?"

"I can come back part time. I need to know when we'll be back from our honeymoon, so I can give her a start date."

"Well, how long would you like to stay at Motel 6?"

I shake my head, "If you take me to Motel 6 for our honeymoon, it will be you getting punished."

He chuckles, "Nothing wrong with Motel 6. They leave the light on for you and everything. That's service."

"Or laziness," I giggle.

"Do you have a passport?" He asks as he strokes my hand.

"I do," I smile. "Where are we going?"

"Somewhere that will have your sexy ass in a gold bikini most of the time."

I roll my eyes, "You really like that one, don't you?"

His gaze darkens, "Oh baby girl, you have no idea."

"Is that a Princess Leia thing?"

He laughs, "No it's not. It's a Mercy thing. I had so many fantasies involving you in that damn bikini."

"Oh really?"

He leans forward and speaks in a low, husky voice.

"Baby girl, my dick is hard as a rock right now simply from thinking about it."

I smirk at him, "What do you plan to do about it?"

He smiles, "Well, I have a heated pool that never gets used. I'm thinking I'd like to go home and see you in it wearing that gold bikini and fuck the hell out of you."

"Don't you have patients to see, Dr. Lexington?"

"I need to be back at two-thirty to meet with a cardiologist. Until then my nurses have it covered."

I stand, "Then stop wasting my time."

He raises an eyebrow as he stands, "One."

We walk out to my car, "I'm driving?"

He nods, "Yes. Your pussy feels good enough I'd risk my life for it."

I gasp, "There's nothing wrong with my driving."

"If you say so, baby girl," he says as he gets into the passenger seat. I get into the driver's seat and drive to the house with Liam stroking my thigh.

"It does make it harder to drive with you doing that."

He slides his hand under my skirt, cupping my pussy, "What about when I do this?"

"Yeah, that doesn't help," I breathe.

Running his fingers up and down the outside of my panties, he hisses, "Fuck, baby girl. You're wet."

I smirk, "Apparently, the effects of the hysterectomy have nothing on you, Daddy."

He slides his fingers inside my panties and rubs my clit. I gasped in surprise, but nothing he does should surprise me anymore.

As I pull into the driveway, he takes his fingers out of my panties and sniffs them as he moans.

"You're so dirty."

"And you fucking love every minute of it."

I smile shyly, "Maybe."

We get out of the vehicle, and he comes around to my side, pushes me up against the car, and places his hands on either side of me.

He runs his tongue from my collarbone to my neck, up to my ear.

"You have exactly five minutes to get into that bikini and into the pool. After that, I cannot be held accountable for my actions."

He bites my neck, "Do you understand, baby girl?"

"Yes, Daddy," I squeak.

"Such a fucking good girl."

He steps back, and I run upstairs to get changed.

I change in the bathroom, brush my hair quickly, and when I leave the bathroom, I'm stopped in my tracks.

"You're naked," I say as I stand gaping at the finest specimen of a man in the world. Not an inch of fat, all hard body, and speaking of hard...his huge cock is completely hard, hanging heavily between his legs, pre-cum leaking. If there is anything hotter, I've never seen it.

His eyes travel up and down my body. At this point, I doubt we'll make it to the pool.

He grabs me by the waist and pulls me into his hard body, staring into my eyes, "You...Are...So... Fucking...Beautiful."

"Thank you," I whisper.

"I've never seen anything as breathtaking as you."

"Liam."

He takes my face in his hands and presses his lips to mine, kissing me deeply. His tongue swirls around mine as he groans. Then he abruptly steps back from me. "Fuck, you make me lose all control. Pool now. I want you in the pool."

"Yes, sir," I smirk and walk to the pool.

"Are people going to see us?"

"No. That's why the privacy wall is there?"

"So you can fuck your women and remain unseen?"

He smacks me on the ass, "Don't start. You are my only woman, and you very well know that."

When he runs up behind me and scoops me into his arms, my heart begins to race. What the hell?

"If you want to be a brat you pay the consequences."

"What?" I gasp.

As we approach the pool, he takes my shoes off and throws them on the pool deck.

"Liam, put me down."

He flashes me an evil grin, "Oh I will put you down, baby girl."

Without any further warning, he tosses me into the pool.

He and his perfect naked body get into the pool as I scowl at him.

He walks toward me in the pool, but I cross my arms over my chest.

"No. Keep your sexy as sin body over there."

He chuckles, enjoying this a little bit. I'm not mad, but I like to play hard-to-get occasionally. And Liam most definitely likes the game of cat and mouse.

"Baby girl," he says as he moves to my side and attempts to corner me. But I swim under the water to the other side of the pool. When I break the surface, he stares at me with a heated gaze as he darts his tongue out and swipes his bottom lip.

"Game...Fucking...On...Baby girl."

Thirty-Two

LIAM

I LOVE when she's in the mood to play. I stalk her, trying to predict her every move. She's quick, but she won't be fast enough. As I approach her, she darts to the side like I knew she would. I grab her hand, but she slips from my grasp with the water. Damn it.

She flashes me a devious grin, "If you catch it, Daddy, it's yours."

"It's mine, either way. And I will catch you. Do you know what I'll do when that happens?"

She shakes her head, "No, what?"

"I'm going to catch you and then I'm going to fuck you until you scream."

A shocked expression appears on her face, "Out here?"

I raise an eyebrow, "Wherever the fuck I want, baby girl. I don't even have a neighbor for half a mile."

She darts to the side and climbs the ladder. I grab her hips and pull her away, "Finders keepers baby girl."

I hear a squeal followed by, "Damn it!"

I pull her to the side with me, and I climb up and sit on the pool's edge.

"Stay in the pool. Are you going to be a good girl for Daddy?"

Her eyes light up, "Yes," she breathes.

I wrap my legs around her back. "Suck my cock."

She stands on her tiptoes and swirls her tongue around my dick.

"Yes, baby girl," I hiss as I stroke her hair.

When she runs her tongue around the head, I shiver. She does this so well, making me crave her.

She lowers her mouth down my length and fuck, she's amazing.

"That feels so good."

Bobbing her head up and down, she moans as she sucks, making me crazy. Every vibration from her mouth takes me closer to the edge. She grabs my balls and gently massages them.

I grab her hair with both hands and drive my cock into her throat, making her gag.

Tears run down her face as I hold her head down, and I release into her beautiful throat.

"Fuck, baby girl, you're so good."

I let her go and wipe the tears that fell on her cheeks and jump in the water.

I pull her bikini top down, exposing her beautiful tits.

"Stunning," I say as I suck her perfect bud into my mouth while cupping the other.

I bite down and then lick her nipple quickly.

"Oh my God," she says breathlessly.

I love how she watches me as I pleasure her. It never gets old.

She runs her hands through my hair while I flick her nipple.

"Yes, Daddy. Oh God."

"I'm going to make you come like this."

I circle her nub with my tongue like I do her clit, and she tips her head back and cries out, "DADDY! FUCK!" as she comes from nipple stimulation. Fuck, she's so Goddamn sexy.

"Let's go," I say.

"Where are we going?"

"Inside where I can spread you out properly and feast on that beautiful pussy of yours."

I pull her out of the pool with me and grab a towel wrapping her in it.

We walk into the house to the bedroom, and I dry off quickly. Taking her towel, I throw it in the hamper.

She grabs the string on her bikini bottoms, and I scowl, "Don't you dare."

Moving her hands away, she says, "Oh."

I grab her, placing my hands on her ass, "Baby girl, I have fantasized about this for far too long. I want the bikini left on."

"Yes, Daddy."

"Good girl. Go lay on the bed with your legs spread."

I grab my cell phone from my pants pocket and stand at the foot of the bed.

"What are you doing?"

"I want a picture of you like this, only for me."

She nods, "Okay."

I take a few pictures, and she says, "Turn your video on."

"What?"

Reluctantly, I do. Not that I wouldn't love a video of her, but I certainly never saw this coming.

I turn my camera on, and she smiles sweetly, as she dips her hand into her bikini bottoms.

"Do you want to see, Daddy?"

"Yes," I reply with heavy breathing.

She takes her hand out and pulls her bottoms to the side, exposing herself to me and the camera.

Knowing she's allowing me to record her like this, has me speechless.

"Take it off," I finally say.

"You wanted it on."

"Take off the bottoms, now."

She unties the sides and removes the bottoms.

I glance at my phone to ensure it's still recording and quickly return my attention to her.

She sucks on her fingers and then starts playing with her pussy.

"Fuck. You're such a good girl. Tell me how it feels, baby girl."

She moans, "It feels so good, Daddy."

I nearly lose my mind when she slips two fingers into her pussy. The sound of her fucking herself taunts me. I want to be inside her now, but I also want to keep filming.

"Add another finger."

She does, and I groan. I move closer and sit on the bed between her legs.

I swipe my fingers up her slit, collecting her arousal on my fingers. I smell my fingers and then taste them.

"You need to come. I'm going to lose control. I need to fuck you, baby girl."

"Then, fuck me," she moans.

I shut the camera off and toss it on the floor. I don't even care about my phone right now.

Turning her on her side, I lift her left leg onto my shoulder and slide into her.

"Fuck," I groan.

I love watching every expression on her face as I fuck her.

"So beautiful."

I smack her ass, and she yells, "HARDER!"

I hit her again, and she smiles, "Thank you, Daddy."

I flip her over and push her legs up by her head.

Gripping her hips, I fuck her hard.

"This fucking pussy is perfect," I growl.

"Daddy," she cries.

She digs her fingers into the sheets as she writhes beneath me.

"Oh my God," she says repeatedly.

"Untie your top for me. Show me your beautiful tits."

She does, and I swear she's the most incredible woman in the world. *The things she does to me.* Being with her is intoxicating.

Her phone rings, and I look at her.

"It can wait," she says.

I reposition myself and hover over her, still moving in and out of my favorite place. I lick her lips before sliding my tongue into her mouth. When I pull away from our kiss, I look at her face, her back arches as she screams during her orgasm, clenching down on my cock, I fill her with my seed.

"Yes, baby girl."

I pull out of her, and she gets up to check her phone, "It was the school."

She calls, and there's no answer.

Mercy starts getting dressed, so I do the same. I didn't know we were in such a hurry, but I guess we are.

She keeps calling the school, but there's no answer.

She's worried. I see it written all over her face.

"Do you want to go to the school?" I ask.

She nods, "Yes, I am concerned."

"Everything is fine, I'm certain. But let's make sure."

I get my shoes on, and she's impatiently waiting by the door.

"Okay, let's go."

We rush out to the car, and she hands me the keys, "I can't drive right now."

I go to open the door, but she snaps at me, "I can open my own fucking door, Liam. Let's go."

"Of course," I say.

I get in quickly, and we drive to the school. Mercy calls the school again and again. While I'm not going to say it, I find it odd that they'd call her and then not answer when she calls back.

We get to the school and park out in front of the entrance. There are so many police cars that it makes my skin crawl. Mercy gasps, but she's on autopilot. She runs to the school, and I turn the car off to go after her. But we have to ring the buzzer to get in. And Mercy is going out of her mind.

"Can I help you?"

"Mercy Madison. Someone called me and then I couldn't get through."

"Come to the office ma'am."

The door clicks, and we both go in.

There are four police officers in the office.

"What's going on?" Mercy asks.

"You're Mercy Madison and you are?" The one officer asks me.

"Dr. Liam Lexington."

"You're Ivy's foster parents, correct?"

"Yes," I respond as Mercy grabs my arm.

"Would you like to sit down, Miss?" He asks.

"No. I'd like to know what's going on," she responds.

He nods, "Ivy was taken from the school playground."

"Taken?" I ask.

"Can you tell me if you know this woman?"

He shows us both a grainy picture on his cell phone."

"That's Ivy's mother, Linda Reynolds," I hiss.

"That's what we thought," he writes something on a notepad."

A sob erupts from Mercy's chest. It turns into a gut-wrenching, piercing cry.

I take her in my arms and hold her.

The officer who has done most of the talking says, "We will find her. We know who has her. I'll be back," he says. He steps outside.

When he comes back, he says, "I have issued an AMBER alert for Ivy. Also, I've gotten an APB on her and the mother."

Mercy says between sobs, "You have to...Find her...She's abusive."

He nods, "We have officers checking her home as well as her last known place of employment. You should both go home, so we know where to find you."

"Come on, babe. Let's do what they say."

I get her into the car and start driving home.

"I need to call the hospital quickly to let them know I'm going to miss the cardiology meeting."

"You can drop me off and go back to work."

I shake my head, "No fucking way. I will not leave you in a time like this."

Thirty-Three

MERCY

LIAM CARRIES me into the house and lays me on the couch. I'm surrounded by darkness, my sweet girl, gone because that bitch decided she wanted her. They took her away because she was not a good mom. In fact, she was abusive. The court decided it wasn't in Ivy's best interest to be there. And now she violates that order and snatches her from the playground. And how could the school let this happen? Someone had to have been on that playground with kids. You don't just allow a bunch of kindergartners to run free without supervision.

My world is spinning, and I feel sick.

"MERCY!"

I shake my head and look up at Liam, "Why are you yelling?"

"I said your name six times, baby. Do you want some tea or anything?"

"No, there's only one thing I want," the tears fall, and I swear I could fill an ocean with them. My chest hurts as if someone smashed it in. The pounding of my heart echoes in my ear drums. "Liam, what if-"?

"Nope. No, what ifs. We aren't doing that."

He sits on the couch and pulls me into his arms, "They are going to find her and soon."

Liam's arms are usually my safe place, but not today. Today there is no safe place. Nothing will make me feel better.

"Do you want to take a bath?"

I shake my head, "Not until she's back."

"I texted Elle, her and Isabella would like to come over."

After a few minutes, he asks, "Is that okay?"

I shrug, "I don't care. It doesn't matter."

I shuffle my body and lay my head down on his lap while he strokes my hair.

"I'm glad you kept the butterflies," I say as I stare at them on the wall.

I sit up and get off the couch, unsure what to do with myself. I pace for a while and then walk to Ivy's room.

I lay down on her bed and held her favorite Elsa stuffy.

Elle and Isabella come in, but I'm facing the wall and have no plans of turning around.

I feel their hands on my back as Elle whispers, "Do you need anything, babe?"

"I just want to be alone."

The weight of the bed shifts as they move off the bed.

"We'll be in the living room if you need anything."

"Baby girl."

"Liam, I need to be alone."

"I thought..." He clears his throat, "Okay, whatever you need."

I know I'm being a terrible friend, and even worse fiancé' but I can't see through my heartbreak.

Ivy is gone, Linda has her, and is doing God knows what to her. Please be safe, sweet girl. I know Ivy is terrified right now, and heartbroken that she isn't with us. What if she kills her? I've heard of horrific things like that happening.

The door is open to the bedroom, and I can hear them talking.

"I don't know what to do. How do I fucking fix this?"

"You can't," Elle says.

"She doesn't even want me around."

"Don't take it personally. She's heartbroken and scared," Isabella adds.

I put my head under Ivy's pillow to block them out.

At some point, I cry myself to sleep. I wake up when I hear footsteps approaching. I look in the doorway.

Liam comes in with a tray of food.

"I'm not hungry."

"Baby girl, you're scaring the hell out of me. Can you eat a few bites and take a couple sips of water?"

"If I do, will you call the police?"

"Yes."

I sit up, and he hands me the tray.

He made my favorite, probably in hopes I would eat it.

I take a forkful of salmon, and it's really good.

After eating about half of it, I eat a few green beans. I can't eat more, so I look at Liam with pleading eyes.

"Thank you, baby girl."

He takes the tray, puts it on the dresser, and sits beside me.

"Just because they say they don't have information doesn't mean they won't find her," he says.

"Liam, just call."

He nods, gets his phone, and pulls out the card from the police officer.

I patiently wait while he asks questions but doesn't give anything away. I feel like snatching the phone out of his hands. But instead, I sit still, wringing my hands like that will somehow give me the answers I desperately need.

He hangs up, and I stare at him impatiently.

Shaking his head, he says, "I'm sorry. She didn't show up for work today. They weren't at her apartment. But they are still looking."

I blow out a big breath, "Can you go please? Close the door behind you."

"Mercy, we are stronger together than we are apart."

"If you prefer it, I will leave," I say.

"Why do I feel like I'm losing both of you?"

I shrug, "If she doesn't come back, I'm not sure there will be anything left of me."

· · ·

169

Five Days Later...

The days turn into nights, the nights turn into days. That's the only thing that happens of consequence. The tears have stopped, and I don't think I have any tears left to cry. Liam is pissed at me or frustrated or whatever. He told me last night that he was tired of me staring at the fucking wall. I'm tired of it too. I'm lost, I can't be motivated, no matter how hard anyone tries. Have you ever felt like you were not even in your body? You were somewhere looking down at your life and watching it happen? That's what it's like. I'm not really here. I hate that I'm hurting the people I love. But I don't know how to stop it. Liam doesn't deserve this; he's got to be hurting too.

Thirty-Four

LIAM

I **WALK** into Ivy's bedroom, fed up with this shit. I know she's upset, but this can't continue any longer. She hasn't had a fucking shower in five days. Being kind and giving her what she thinks she needs is not working. I've always known what she needs. Why on earth I second-guessed myself, I don't know.

"Get up."

"Liam go."

"Nope, we are done with this shit. You're taking a shower. Get the fuck up before I pick you up."

"I just want to be alone," she tucks herself into the corner.

"Okay. Have it your way, baby girl." I scoop her up and carry her to the bathroom in my bedroom.

When I set her on her feet, I can start the shower, while she stands with her arms crossed and a scowl on her face.

"Take your clothes off."

She rolls her eyes at me but gets undressed.

"Good girl."

I get the temperature right and get undressed.

She gasps, "I'm not having sex with you."

"That's fine. It's just a shower. Just because we've never done that doesn't mean we are incapable."

I wave for her to get in and then get in after her.

"Tilt your head back."

"I can wash my own hair."

"Would you just let me fucking take care of you?"

"Fine," she huffs.

I don't know where the hell my sweet Mercy is but fuck if I don't want her back.

I get her hair wet and squirt some shampoo into my hand, lathering her hair. She closes her eyes and instantly relaxes in front of me.

She's not the only one who feels relaxed. I have barely been able to touch my girl for five days. I miss her. Sleeping alone has been torture.

After I rinse her hair, she gives me the slightest smile and says quietly, "Thank you."

Then I wash her body. I've been craving having her next to me. It's not about sex, even though I am used to having sex every day, multiple times. It's her. I just need my girl with me. It's been a lonely existence.

We get out of the shower, and I dry her off.

"Lay on the bed on your stomach."

She raises her eyebrow, "Liam."

"Tonight, I'm taking care of you. You're so tense. I'm going to give you a massage."

I put boxer shorts on, walked over to the bed, and straddled her hips without putting any weight on her.

She moans as I massage her shoulders, "That feels so good."

About ten minutes later, my beautiful girl is sleeping in my bed, where she belongs.

I cover her with the blankets and go to make myself a drink, which I intend to bring to the bedroom. I can watch her and make sure she is okay. Something is comforting about watching her sleep.

I take a sip of my drink and hear a knock at the door.

I nearly sprint to the door so whoever it is doesn't wake Mercy up. My girl is exhausted.

Opening the door, I cannot believe my eyes.

"Dr. Lexington."

Ivy is standing in front of me. I can't even believe it.

"I'm sorry, I'm not dressed. Come in." I grab Ivy and hug her tight, "I'll be right back. I'm going to get Mercy up."

I go to the bedroom, pull on pajama pants and a t-shirt and get Mercy's robe.

"Baby girl, get up. Put your robe on."

"Why?"

"The police are here."

She literally jumps out of bed and puts her robe on.

We walk out, and when she sees Ivy, she starts sobbing. Ivy runs to her and grabs onto her for dear life.

Mercy picks her up, takes her to the couch, and cradles her in her arms.

"Are you okay?" She asks.

Ivy erupts in tears, "I'm okay. I thought I would never see you again."

The police officer glances at me, "We are going to need to have her come to the station to give a statement, but I felt like this reunion couldn't wait."

"Thank you," I say.

"She kept talking about Mercy before we even left the motel she was at."

"Was she hurt?"

He shakes his head, "We will see what we find out in the interview but at this point it doesn't seem like it."

I run a hand through my hair as I watch Ivy and Mercy talk to the officer.

"Please tell me you arrested her."

"We did. And with her rap sheet bail is unlikely."

My eyes snap to his, "Rap sheet?"

"Yeah, mostly drug and prostitution related offenses."

"This interview can't be done here?"

He shakes his head, "I'm sorry."

I walk over to Mercy and sit beside her, "We have to take her to the police station, they need to interview her."

Mercy glares at me, "Liam."

"I know, baby girl. Let's get this over with and then we'll bring her home where she belongs."

I glance back to the officer who seems to be in charge, "Can she ride with us?"

He nods, "Of course."

After we both get dressed, we all get in the car and drive to the police station.

Mercy sits in the back with Ivy holding on to her and not wanting to let go.

"Did I miss the wedding?" Ivy asks.

Mercy smiles the first real smile I've seen in nearly a week, "No, sweet girl."

"I can't wait to try on my dress."

"Tomorrow, sweet girl. No school. We will go try on your dress, get our nails done, maybe go shopping. How does that sound?"

Ivy squeals, "Yayyy!"

They both groan in displeasure as we pull up to the police station.

We walk in together, Ivy and Mercy, hand in hand.

The officer in charge comes and gets us and sets Ivy up in a room. Mercy makes it clear she's not planning on leaving.

He looks at her and says, "I know this has been a terrible ordeal. And if you insist on staying in with her, I won't fight you. But we're much more likely to get the information we need without you there. Honestly, it will likely be less emotional for her if you're not. You can stand outside and watch through the glass."

Much to my surprise, she nods and walks over to Ivy, "I'll be right outside. After you're done, we will go home and put you in your favorite princess pajamas."

She hugs her and comes back to me, takes my hand, and we go to watch through the glass.

A female walks in and sits on a couch with Ivy. This room is different from the interrogation room I was in. Softer.

A man comes up to us and presses a button on the glass, and we can hear inside the room. He walks away.

"Hi Ivy, I'm Sheila. I'm a detective here."

"Hi. What's a detec-," Ivy responds.

"It's a special kind of police officer." She smiles at Ivy, "I need to ask you a few questions about what happened, is that okay? Can you tell me what happened at school?"

Ivy sits, twisting her fingers on her lap, "With my mom?"

Sheila nods.

"I was playing tag with my friends. My mom came up to the fence and called me over."

She looks down, "She opened the fence and told me Mercy had a bad accident. I had to go with her so she could take me to her."

I put my arm around Mercy when she begins to sob.

"The fence wasn't locked?"

"No."

"So, you left with her?"

Ivy nods.

"Where was your teacher?"

"Timmy fell off the slide. He never listens. You aren't supposed to stand at the top of the slide. It's not safe."

"That's right. Where did your mom take you?" Sheila sits listening to Ivy with her notebook, writing down all the details even though it's being recorded.

"A hotel."

"Did she say why?"

"She told me we would sleep there at night and go see Mercy in the morning."

"Did she hurt you?"

Ivy shakes her head, "Mean words. But no hitting."

"Why did she say mean words?"

"She wanted me to go live with her. But I want to live with Mercy and Liam."

"Tell me about them."

She glows, "Mercy is my best friend. We paint together, play dress up, Barbies, we do everything. And Liam used to be Dr. L. He was my cancer doctor. I love him too. He wore princess clothes for me. He made me not sick anymore."

I swallow down the lump in my throat.

She continues, "There's going to be a wedding. I get to wear a pretty dress."

"You do?" She asks excitedly.

Ivy nods, "Yep. I love pretty dresses."

"Your mom told you Mercy was in an accident?"

"Yeah. She said if Mercy died, I'd have to go live with her."

Mercy cries more, I kiss her on the top of her head, "It's okay, baby girl, she's safe now."

"That must have been scary."

"I cried. Mom got angry but didn't hit me."

"I would've cried too," the detective says.

"I don't want Mercy to die. I was scared and wanted to go see her right away but mom said no."

"Did you eat?"

Ivy laughs, "I'm used to big meals now. Mercy cooks a lot of food. I'm still hungry. Mom gave me a peanut butter sandwich."

"Do you like Mercy's cooking?"

She scrunches up her nose, "Most of it. She makes me eat carrots, and green beans. I don't like them."

Mercy laughs, "Her and those damn carrots."

"Do you eat them?"

Ivy nods, "Sometimes we get to make cookies when I eat what she gives me."

"Oh, I love chocolate chip cookies."

Ivy squeals, "Me too. Mercy makes the best cookies."

She smiles at Ivy, "Is there anything else that happened with your mom we should know about?"

"No. She said mean words. She doesn't like Mercy."

She nods, "Okay. If you remember anything else Mercy and Liam will have my phone number, so you can call me."

Ivy nods, "Can I go home now?"

"You sure can. We might come visit you soon, okay?"

Ivy beams, "I will show you my princess room. It's got princesses on the wall. And the bed. And lots of princess toys."

She giggles, "That sounds lovely, Ivy. I can't wait to see it."

The detective brings Ivy out to us, and she immediately jumps into Mercy's arms.

She hands me a card, "Call me if she remembers anything else."

I nod, "Thank you."

We walk out of the police station and head home.

Thirty-Five

MERCY

AFTER GETTING her some proper dinner, we got her into her pajamas, *Frozen* ones, of course, and put her to bed. We walk out of her bedroom together, and Liam asks if I want wine, and after the last five days, I definitely do.

I sit on the couch, and Liam comes in and hands me a glass of wine.

"We need to talk," I said after taking a gulp of my wine and setting it on the coffee table.

He nods and sits beside me.

I blow out a big breath, "I'm sorry."

He stares at me in surprise, "For what?"

I laugh, "Liam, I'm aware that I've been the worst fiancé' any man has ever had. I didn't know how to deal with her being taken from us. I was so worried about what was happening to her. I was so lost in my own devastation, that I ignored yours."

"Baby girl, I would not have expected you to know how to deal with that. You were not easy to handle. But I'm not sure I would've imagined you would react any differently. I do wish you would have turned to me instead of away from me. Still, I can't blame you for reacting in a negative way."

He sets his wine glass on the table beside mine, "If I don't kiss you right now, I'm going to lose my mind. It's been five fucking days. Let me kiss you."

I smirk at him, "Wow. Are you asking permission, Dr. Lexington? It seems you've lost your edge."

"Dirty girl, I have most definitely not lost my edge."

He grabs me by my hair, pulls my lips to his, and kisses me with a hard, bruising kiss, it's all lips and teeth clashing, with an urgency I've never seen from him.

When he pulls back, he picks me up, carrying me over his shoulder to the bedroom.

He sets me down and immediately starts undressing me.

Cupping both of my breasts, he says, "I don't just want you, baby girl. I fucking need you. Five days without you is too long."

I pull his Henley up and over his head. And then help him out of his jeans. When he shimmies out of his boxers, I gasp.

I run my hands all over his chest, "You're so hot."

He chuckles, "No, baby girl, that's all you."

I gaze into his eyes, "Fuck me like you own me, Dr. Lexington."

He picks me up and lays me on the bed, pulling my ass to the edge of the bed.

Sliding into me, he groans, "Jesus. Fuck."

He grips both of my hips and slams into me over and over.

"You feel so fucking good. Baby girl, you're so good."

I grab his nipples and twist them, "Tell me you missed this."

"Baby girl, miss isn't the right fucking word. It was agony. You were so close yet so far. I watched that fucking video a thousand times."

The sound of our skin slapping together fills the room, and a sheen of sweat covers his perfect body, making him look even sexier than normal.

"This perfect pussy is mine."

"Yes," I moan.

He leans over me, "Put your arms around my neck."

Lifting me off the bed, he moves his hands under my ass and moves me up and down his cock with an awe-inducing amount of strength.

"Come for me, baby girl."

His breathing is heavy as perspiration rolls down his chest.

I dig my hands into his shoulders as my climax gets closer.

He's slamming into me with blinding force.

"Dirty sluts come for their Daddy's when told."

I wrap my arms around his neck and bury my face in his chest as my orgasm ripples through me with such strength that I swear I can feel it from my head to my toes.

"Ahhhh!" I yell as he slams twice more before he groans through his orgasm.

He sets me down on the floor, holding me closer to him, and strokes my hair.

"You're so perfect, baby girl. I love everything about you."

After a shower, we lay in bed talking about everything.

"I think we should find a surrogate soon."

"Not until Ivy is at least in the process of being adopted," I said.

"I'll talk to the lawyer about that tomorrow," he says softly rubbing my back.

"I'm working in the morning tomorrow," he says and then adds, "I have to meet Xander for lunch, he's freaking out."

"Why?" I ask.

"Apparently, someone got into the house when no one was there and stole Isabella's worn underwear from the laundry basket."

I gasp, "The stalker."

"Probably. Who else would do something like that?"

"I know Max will be with you if Elle is around. But if Isabella is there, I want you to be extra careful. Promise me. I can't lose you, baby girl."

I sigh, "I promise. I'll be keenly aware of my surroundings."

"Good girl," he kisses me on the forehead.

"Now sleep."

* * *

I wake up in the morning feeling refreshed. I don't think I moved all night long. When I look to my left, I notice the empty bed beside me. So, I get up, put on my robe, and search for my little family. Liam and Ivy are in the kitchen cooking.

Ivy squeals, "We made you breakfast!"

"You did?" I ask excitedly.

"We made blueberry muffins and some fruit, because Liam said you don't like a heavy breakfast."

I smile, "He's right."

We sit eating, and Ivy says, "Can you eat faster?"

I raise an eyebrow, "Excuse me?"

"I wanna go. I've been waiting forever."

"Go get dressed. Make sure you match. Blues with blues. Reds with reds."

She rolls her eyes, "I know what match means."

After she goes to her room, I say, "I might be ready to drop her off at school by noon."

Liam chuckles, "Today will be good for you two."

I nod, "Yes, it will be. I'm looking forward to pampering the sassy little Princess."

"Should I call my dad about Isabella?"

He shakes his head, "I already owe him a favor."

I wag my finger at him, "No you don't. He can consider letting Nash live a favor to me. You will never be involved with the shit my dad is, Liam. I won't allow it. I would never marry one of his thugs."

"If you want to call your dad then you should. But they have to find proof that it was him."

"Doesn't Xander have cameras? What's better than video proof?"

"The camera feed was cut."

Ivy comes out wearing a cute red dress with matching red shoes. And the smile on her face is priceless.

"Give me five minutes. I just need to get dressed."

I run and get dressed as quickly as possible. After I brush my teeth and hair, I put my shoes on and find Ivy waiting impatiently.

I give her an impatient look, "Are you ready yet? I've been waiting for you!"

She glares at me, "MERCY! I've been waiting for YOU!"

Liam chuckles.

I walk over to him and kiss him quickly, "I love you. Have a good day."

"What about Elle and Isabella?"

"They will meet us there, as well as Max."

He nods, "Xander is picking me up shortly because he's going to the hospital and my Escalade is still there."

"Ok, babe. See you later."

Ivy quickly hugs him and kisses his cheek, "Bye, Liam!"

We get into the car, and this girl bounces on her damn seat like the energizer bunny.

When we pull up to the bridal shop, she undoes her seatbelt.

"Ivy! You know better. If the car is still moving at all, your seatbelt stays on! And how did you learn that?"

I'm not pleased to find she can get out of her booster seat.

"Sorry," she huffs.

I go around to the back and get her out.

She puts her little hand in mine, and we walk into the bridal shop together. Isabella, Elle, and of course, Max, are already there.

She runs off and hugs everyone.

The shop owner comes up and hugs me.

"It's good to see you again. This must be Ivy."

I smile, "It is."

"Well let's try on this pretty dress."

Ivy runs behind her, 'pretty dress' is all she needed to hear.

I help Ivy with the dress once she gets her clothes off.

I zip it up in the back, and she starts yelling as she looks in the mirror.

"Oh my. It's so beautiful! Isn't it beautiful?"

I smile behind her, "It's very beautiful."

Stella says, "Come look in the big mirror!"

We walk out and everybody, even Max ooh's and ahh's about my pretty princess.

She spins around gleefully.

This right here is a moment for the memory books. She's laughing, smiling, and as far as she's concerned, she's wearing the most beautiful dress in the world.

"Can I wear this every day?"

Everybody laughs.

"That's just for the wedding," Elle says.

I add, "But, we'll have a picture taken on our wedding day and put it in your bedroom so you can always see it."

She beams at me, "My friend Sophie at school is adopted. She had an adoption party and wore a pretty dress. Maybe I could wear it for my adoption party."

I can't help it, I take her into my arms, "I think that would be lovely, sweet girl."

I swallow the lump in my throat and hope we can make this happen for her.

We let her wear the dress for a few minutes before telling her to get changed. Eventually, I had no choice. She'd stay here all day if it meant keeping the dress on.

"Okay, we have to get you changed, we have a spa appointment for your nails."

The swanky spa we are going to is two doors down, so we walk. Keeping my promise, I look around and stay aware of things around me. We go into the Luxe Boutique Nail and Spa, and all sit at different stations to get our nails done. I instruct Maria, who is doing Ivy's nails, that it needs to be a neutral color. Pink is okay, light, absolutely no red. I'm pretty sure Liam would lose his shit.

She decides on a pinkish pearl color which is fine with me and quite pretty. This place is amazing, when we finish our manicures, we start our pedicures. They bring lunch while we have our pedicures. It's just sandwiches and pickles, but it's delicious. Ivy loves the pickles and asks for everyone. Look, I love the girl, but she's not getting my fucking pickle. Ivy is enamored with the lady beside her, she's getting a Fish Pedicure. Literally, a bunch of fish known as Doctor Fish are in the water with her feet. They should call it a Kardashian Pedicure. Anyway, it's a little much for me. I'm not putting my feet in fish water. Ivy won't leave the lady alone.

"Does it hurt?"

"Oh my God, that one is going to bite you."

"Does it tickle?"

"Can they smell feet?"

"Do you know fish can't live out of water?"

"Ivy, would you leave her alone?" I said.

She laughs, "It's okay."

"What if the smell of her feet kills the fish?"

"Oh my God, Ivy, stop."

Well, that's one less spa I can go to in the future. But Elle and Isabella think it's hilarious.

"We should all get fish pedicures the day before the wedding," Elle says.

I shake my head, "Let's not and say we did."

Elle appears distraught, "You're the oldest young person I've ever met."

"Hey now, I have done adventurous things."

Isabella laughs so hard she snorts, "Yeah, your best friend's dad."

I give Isabella a look, I don't want Ivy hearing that. We finish and walk out to the car to go home.

I glance at Elle, "Can you put Ivy in the car for me?"

"I'd love to," she yells as she tickles Ivy.

I go up to Isabella, "Hey, Liam told me what happened."

Max watches Elle closely but physically stays closer to Isabella, which is interesting.

"Yeah, embarrassing," she says.

"Has anything else happened?"

"No."

"Look, you need to be careful. This guy is escalating, Isabella. I think you should hire security."

She smiles at Max, "We share Max."

"Not enough. Max is one man with one set of eyes. Think about it, please."

"I will," she says.

"He's not going to stop, Isabella. Not until he's either in prison or gets what he wants from you, whatever the hell that is."

"Mercy, I get it," she bites.

But I don't think she does. For some reason, I don't think Isabella is thinking about how horrible this could get. The end result could be that he takes her life. She needs to act before that happens.

I hug her, "I just want you to be okay."

"I know. Love you."

"Love you too. Text you later."

I walk over to Elle and hug her, "Text me later, alright?"

She nods, "She doesn't listen to anybody, it's not just you."

I get into the car and drive Ivy home. It's been a long day filled with excitement, and it's about five minutes before she crashes in the car.

Thirty-Six

MERCY

THE WEDDING DAY...

Last night we stayed at a hotel, Me, Elle, Isabella, Ivy, and Max. Max had an adjoining room but checked on us every hour whether he heard any commotion or not.

Ivy is in the chair, getting her makeup done. I've instructed Reuben, the makeup artist, to keep her makeup minimal and very natural.

He's already done everyone else's makeup. We saved Ivy for last since she's the one most likely to smudge it. She's sitting patiently, knowing that she'll put on her dress next.

When he finishes, he yells, "Magnificent!" As he did with all the rest of us. He's a little over the top but very talented just the same.

As he leaves, he says, "Tell Dr. Liam, I said congratulations."

After he leaves, Elle and Isabella crack up laughing.

"Oh stop," I said.

It's no secret to any of us that Reuben wants my Liam. I'd cut a bitch, besides he's lacking the right parts for my man. When we had the consultation with him, he spent the entire hour eye-fucking Liam.

Ivy yells, "Is it time? Is it time?"

I laugh, "It's time."

Elle takes my arm, "Are you doing, okay? Any jitters?"

"I've been in love with your brother since I was sixteen years old. I'm ready for this. No jitters, not a one."

She smiles sweetly, "Let's get your gown on."

I nod.

In order not to mess up my hair and makeup, Elle very carefully puts the gown over my head, while Isabella helps Ivy get dressed.

She moves to the front of me after zipping my dress up.

"My God, Mercy, you look so beautiful. My brother is going to lose his mind."

I giggle, "I hope so."

The dress I picked is made of Italian silk but has a lace overlay. The plunging neckline will be what makes Liam crazy. I'm sure of it. The back is cut out into a 'V' with a chapel-length train.

Ivy comes over and stares at me as if I'm a Disney Princess come to life.

"You look like a princess," she says.

"Thank you, sweet girl."

I smile, "I have something for you."

I reach into my bag on the couch and pull out the small tiara I had made for her.

After securing the tiara on her head, she looks in the mirror and squeals.

"All princesses need tiaras, right?"

She nods with unshed tears in her eyes. "Thank you."

"You're welcome, beautiful girl."

After everyone is ready, it's time to go to the Butterfly Conservatory.

We all take a limo, which I think is a little over the top, but Liam was insistent. I know he wanted to spoil me, and make me happy, so I gave in.

My phone chimes as we drive.

I get it out of my clutch, turn off the ringer and open a text message from Liam.

Daddy: I love you, baby girl. Don't chicken out.

I roll my eyes.

Me: Oh Daddy, I wouldn't dream of it. 🔪👺🐼

I grin like a Cheshire cat as I put my phone away.

"I need to ditch Max and find me a man that makes me smile stupidly like that," Elle says.

I raise an eyebrow, "Max keeps you safe."

"He also keeps the men away," she mutters dryly.

"True," I say because it is. And it's got to suck to be watched twenty-four hours a day. Max is a big, burly guy, and of course, any man will steer clear of her when he's around and he's always around. He's rather intimidating.

We finally get to the venue, and my heart starts pounding. The next time I see Liam, we will be saying our vows.

We pull up beside the entrance, and everyone gets out before me. Max helps me out last, by holding the back of my dress, so it doesn't get dirty.

I smile at him, "Thank you, Max."

"My pleasure," he says with a stoic expression.

Ivy is spinning around, squealing, "We're here. Oh my God, I love it here so much."

"Ivy, please don't fall and mess up your dress." I look at Isabella, "You're sure Xander has the rings?"

She rolls her eyes, "For the twentieth time yes, Bridezilla, Xander has everything."

I nod, "Sorry."

Elle gets all the flowers out of the trunk, hands each of us our bouquets and Ivy her basket of rose petals.

We walk inside to the rose garden where our ceremony is being held. Liam hired a harpist for the music since they aren't set up for anything else here. Xander comes out and smiles at me.

"Doc Delicious is getting married," he chuckles. "You look stunning, Mercy," he kisses me on the cheek.

"Thank you."

The music starts, and he says, "Alright, ladies. That's us."

He walks into the rose garden with Elle on his left arm and Isabella on his right.

"You're next, Ivy. Do you remember what to do?"

She beams at me, "Yup!"

Max glances at me, "I will make sure she gets in okay and then take my seat."

"Thank you. You really are wonderful."

He blushes a little and averts my gaze, clearly uncomfortable with compliments, "Congratulations, Mercy."

"Thank you," I smile shyly.

Max takes Ivy's hand escorting her to the rose garden.

Suddenly, both doors open as my song is played. I take a deep breath. I decided not to invite my parents because I didn't want my dad around Liam. It made sense at the time, but at this moment, I feel very alone. I know I want to marry him. There's no doubt, but this is kind of scary. I hope I don't fall.

My nerves are getting to me as I walk to the door. Once inside the rose garden, I glance up and spot Liam staring at me, his hand over his heart, his expression one of adoration.

I force myself to walk slowly and not run to him.

When I get to him, he takes my hands in his and stares at me with awe.

"You look so beautiful," he whispers.

The minister starts speaking about love, marriage, and commitment. But I'm having trouble concentrating because all I see is Liam.

After we say our vows and exchange rings, the minister speaks.

"This moment in time is truly a cause for joyous celebration, for we are gathered here to witness not only the beginning of a new marriage, but also the beginning of a new family.

Liam and Mercy would like to take this moment to recognize the significant role that Ivy Reynolds plays in this marriage celebrated today by presenting her with a gift."

Xander hands me the bracelet we had made for Ivy. It's rose gold with butterflies and roses alternating in a row.

I speak to Ivy, who now stands between us with a confused look.

"Ivy, you know that we are trying to adopt you because we want you to be part of our family forever. Regardless of what the courts decide, we are family, our bond has been created and can never be destroyed. No matter what anybody says, you are our daughter."

I put the bracelet on her wrist.

Liam squats down to her level, looks back and forth at us, and nearly yells, "Can I call you mom and dad then?"

All of our guests laugh.

Liam and I both reply, "Yes," at the same time.

She hugs Liam, and it's as if she's thanking him a thousand times just for loving her.

He speaks low to her, "Go stand with Elle we are almost done and ready to go party."

She does, and the minister smiles.

"Throughout this ceremony, Liam and Mercy have vowed, in our presence, to be loyal and loving towards each other. They have formalized the existence of the bond between them, with words spoken, and with the giving and receiving of rings. Therefore, it is my pleasure to pronounce them husband and wife. You may kiss your bride."

Liam takes me in his arms and kisses me like no one is watching. After hearing the hoots and hollers from our friends, he finally pulls away, and the minister announced us, "Ladies and Gentlemen, I present to you Dr. and Mrs. Liam Lexington,"

We rented a hotel suite for a small reception, so we head back there for the celebration.

This time it's just Liam and me in our limo and the rest of our friends and Ivy in the other. He hands me a glass of champagne, "For my beautiful wife."

I giggle, "That sounds weird."

"Get used to it, baby girl. Tonight, I'll make you mine for the rest of our lives."

"Tonight? We are already married," I say after drinking a sip of champagne.

He brushes the hair out of my face, "Baby girl, I've never been inside my wife. Tonight, I will be, and you will completely be mine."

I shake my head, "I've been yours since I was sixteen."

We make it up to the hotel suite, and I see Elle and Isabella did a wonderful job decorating. There are flowers everywhere with fairy lights strung throughout.

The DJ announces, "Ladies and Gentlemen make way for Dr. and Mrs. Liam Lexington."

He starts playing, 'Better Today' by Coffey Anderson.

Liam pulls me into his arms, and we dance.

"I changed my mind about dancing," he whispers.

"Is that so?"

"Oh, baby girl, if you're in my arms, it can't be so bad."

He kisses me, and we stop moving.

Elle yells, "That's not dancing. That's making out."

He pulls back from me and glares at her.

"Little sisters are fucking annoying."

When we start dancing again, I notice Xander dancing with Ivy off to the side.

He kisses my neck and whispers to me, "I love you so fucking much."

I giggle, "I love you too."

We dance the night away.

My 'I don't dance man' even danced with Ivy, bringing me to tears.

I love my little family. It's everything I've ever wanted.

Thirty-Seven

LIAM

"I'M ready to take my wife upstairs," I say to Mercy.

She smiles, "I thought you'd never ask."

We say goodbye to everybody. Ivy grabs onto Mercy and whines, "I'm going to miss you."

"We will talk every day, sweet girl. Besides, you're going to have so much fun with Aunt Elle."

It's hard for Mercy to walk away from her, but she manages.

When we get into the room, Mercy gasps, "It's beautiful."

The living room has a large L-shaped black couch with candles throughout. There's a bar with champagne, strawberries, and dipping chocolate on the bar. She spots the box beside the champagne.

"What's this?" She asks.

"Open it and see."

She does and glances at me with a smirk, "Cupcakes?"

"I happen to know what you can do with a cupcake, baby girl."

She blushes, and it makes my cock twitch.

I grab her waist, "Baby girl, as beautiful as you look in this dress, I'm dying to see what's underneath."

"Help yourself, Dr. Lexington."

I growl as I reach behind her and unzip her dress.

It takes work, but I get it over her hips, and it drops to the floor.

I stand back, gaping at her like a virginal teenager. She's so fucking beautiful.

"Fuck, baby girl."

She's standing in front of me wearing an ivory corset, low cut, her fucking tits spilling out the top. Thigh highs are attached with garter straps, she's got panties on that are lacy, but I can see her pussy lips through them. And fuck me, I'm not sure I could speak if I tried. Her outfit is completed with sparkly ivory-colored stilettos.

"You make me wet when you look at me like that," she says.

I just keep staring at her as if I've never seen her in a state of undress.

She giggles, "Are you okay?"

"No. There's about a million things I want to do to you, and I'm trying to decide where to start."

I grab her, lift her in my arms, bridal style, and carry her to the bedroom.

When I set her on her feet, I grab her face and kiss her like she's the air I breathe. Fuck, maybe she is.

"When I saw you in my bathroom, I wanted you so bad I could taste it. When you came into my office, I wanted you even more. When you snuck into my room, I knew I had to have you. But right now? I've never wanted you more than I do right now."

I drop to my knees and kiss her exposed thighs.

"Spread your legs, baby girl."

She does, and I suck her clit through her thin panties. Then I pull them to the side and run my tongue up her slit repeatedly. She grabs onto my hair, moaning, pushing her pussy into my face.

"Do you like that, baby girl?"

"Yes, Daddy. YES!"

"Good girl."

I attack her clit with my tongue, flicking it as quickly as possible.

"I'm going to come quickly if you keep that up."

I growl and keep going at the same pace.

Stopping for a second, I say, "You may be my wife now. But nothing has changed. In the bedroom you're still my dirty fucking slut. So, give it to me. Be a good girl. Come for Daddy."

I suck her clit hard, and she explodes in my mouth, screaming obscenities.

Standing up, I say, "I need you out of this."

I unbutton the corset of a million buttons. I unclasp the thigh highs and tosses the corset on the floor.

"Baby girl, I think you look even better like this. Leave the shoes and thigh highs on." She takes her panties off while giggling, "Yes, sir."

I take my shirt off and kick off my shoes. My impatient wife reaches forward and unbuttons my belt and pants. Next, she unzips my pants and yanks them with my boxers to the floor.

"In a hurry?" I ask with a raised eyebrow.

"Yes," she says.

I pick her up and toss her on the bed.

"Spread those beautiful thighs."

I climb over her and slide into her.

She moans loudly, which I love, every single moan is like music to my ears.

I pick up my speed, and she runs her nails down my back and wraps her legs around my waist.

"Harder, Daddy, fuck me harder. Please."

Holding myself up on my knuckles, I slam into her best in this position.

"You're so perfect for me. Such a dirty slut."

I get up and grab her hips so I can hit her harder.

I slam into her, watching her tits bounce and her head hit the pillow repeatedly.

"YES!" She yells.

I run my hand down her abdomen, every inch of her is perfect in my eyes.

"Baby girl, you need to come."

She pushes me flat onto my back and rides me. What the hell just happened? Where's my submissive girl?

That thought flies out of my head when she starts fucking me like a wild animal. She bounces up and down faster than a speeding bullet.

I grab her nipples and pinch them. She throws her head back, screaming out her orgasm. It's not long before I'm right there with her.

We both move back to the head of the bed, and I take her in my arms.

"I think I like being married," she says.

I laugh, "Me too, baby."

"Some people might say we have sex too much," she says.

"Fuck them. I never liked them anyway. Too much sex? That's the stupidest thing I've ever heard."

She giggles, "I love you."

I kiss her on the forehead, "I love you too, baby girl. This is only the beginning."

Liam and Mercy: The Wedding Night, Honeymoon and Beyond...

Read on for and excerpt of the next book in this series.

They open my bag in the middle of the airport and rifle through it. Mercy looks at me, "What the hell is in the bag?"

I blow out a big breath, "Fuck. I should've put it in the checked baggage."

Mercy looks nervous. She probably thinks I have a gun in there.

"What's this?" The female guard asks.

She's holding a pink butt plug in the air much to my displeasure. People in line behind us snicker. Mercy has an expression that says she might kill me. And I'd like to strangle this woman. Seriously, everybody knows what a butt plug is. Don't they?

"It's a butt plug." I say simply.

"Is it yours?"

"Yeah, sure it's mine." I roll my eyes.

She puts it back into the bag and allows us to go. I guess she's done trying to humiliate us. It didn't bother me, it's a butt plug, no big deal. But I can tell from looking at my wife for her it is a very big deal. I don't think I'll hear the end of this for a while.

We finally board our plane, and we sit at the front, in first class. Her excitement about where we are traveling is long gone and replaced with anger.

"What kind of a fucking idiot doesn't pack that in a suitcase instead of a carry-on bag?" She asks.

I sigh, "Someone whose wife packed enough clothes for six months so there was no room left in said suitcase."

"Well, I'm so sorry I want to look nice."

"You'd look nice in a butt plug and ball gag. That takes up far less space too."

She glares at me, "In your dreams."

I chuckle. She's so damn cute when she's mad.

I kiss her on the neck, and she sighs loudly.

"I'm still mad at you."

I whisper in her ear so only she can hear me, "Baby girl, when I fuck you so hard that you can't remember your own name you will forget this too."

"When will that be?" She asks with a smirk.

"Five minutes after we check in."

"Maybe, I'll forgive you then."

I take my finger and thumb and place them on her chin, tilting her head up to look me in the eyes.

"Don't be a brat. You know what happens."

She glares at me, "What?"

I've had about enough of her bad attitude.

"Ever heard of edging, baby girl?"

She shakes her head.

"I think tonight you'll be introduced to it."

She raises an eyebrow in confusion.

"We haven't taken off. Google it."

She does and then murmurs, "It doesn't sound like a punishment."

I grin, "It will be torture until I allow you to come. You'll see. Baby girl, you'll be begging me for an orgasm."

She puts her phone away and stares out the window, more annoyed with me than ever. But that's okay.

I whisper to her, "Daddy, always wins baby girl."

Acknowledgments

Thank you for reading Finding Mercy which was supposed to be a stand alone but after falling in love with Liam and Mercy so much I had to write more.

To my ARC readers thank you for choosing to read my book when there are so many choices out there!

To my editor... I adore you. Thank you.

Jasmine and Chanel my PA's... You put up with an extra special level of crazy. Thank you.

About the Author

Chelle Rose is an American author of smut books with a plot. They tend to be heavy on angst, and just when you think there can't possibly be another sex scene, there is! She tends to favor the forbidden trope but doesn't hold herself to it.

Also by Chelle Rose

Hard to Love

Hard to Breathe

Coming Soon!

Liam and Mercy: The Wedding Night, The Honeymoon and Beyond...
Releasing October 1, 2022!

Releasing December 1, 2022!

Book Four of the Forbidden Desires of PCH Series

Xander's Secret

Cover coming soon!

Blurb:

Bro code rule number one...

You don't fuck your best friends sister. Ever.

After the worst time in my life she's the one that never left my side. I started to notice things about her I never did before. The way her eyes drop to my lips when I speak, the sultry low tone of her voice. And damn it, the way every curve of her body calls my name in a bikini.

She's an angel with the body of a goddess. I need her more than my next breath.

But I can't have her. Not now, not ever. But...

What if I can't control myself? What if just once I give into what I need so desperately?